BOWERBIRDS

NESTED HEARTS BOOK TWO

ADA MARIA SOTO

ROOKERY

Published by
Rookery Publishing
PO Box 300280, Albany, Auckland, 0752, New Zealand
http://rookerypublishing.com/

This is a work of fiction. Names, characters, places, and incidents either are the product of author imagination or are used fictitiously, and any resemblance to actual persons, living or dead, business establishments, events, or locales is entirely coincidental.

Bowerbirds First Edition (published by Dreamspinner Press)

© 2015 Ada Maria Soto

Bowerbirds Second Edition

© 2020 Ada Maria Soto

Cover Art

© 2015 Paul Richmond.

http://www.paulrichmondstudio.com

ISBN: 978-0-473-51850-9 [Paperback]

ISBN: 978-0-473-51851-6 [epub]

ISBN: 978-0-473-51852-3 [kindle]

ISBN: 978-0-473-51853-0 [ibooks]

Acknowledgments

This book would literally not exist without Cooper West.

CONTENTS

AUTHOR'S NOTE

SECOND EDITION

Bowerbirds has always been a slightly odd book for be since it was the book that wasn't supposed to happen. Empty Nests was one giant book, and I do mean giant. 130,000 words which is way too long for any sensible romance novel and yet I could not get my characters to speed up. They didn't believe in love or even lust at first sight and had far too many personal anxieties to allow things to go smooth. I was very close to deleting the whole thing when I sent it to Cooper West in a last-ditch cry for help. She bought me a copy of Scrivener, told me to flip two scenes in the middle, and cut it into two books.

I've had a few people in the following years tell me I should have kept it as one book, and just as many say it was fine as two and they wanted a third. Any which way it's far too late to change that now. I have added a short epilogue onto this. It was originally published as a short story for my newsletter at a time when my newsletter had twenty subscribers.

This book takes place in 2011 (the year I started writing it) when it was still sort of possible to do big international business in Russia.

Several real places and organizations are named or appear in this book. No money or gifts have changed hands. In fact, they would probably be surprised to find themselves here.

April 10, 2011
  N 37° 47' 06.8", W 122° 23' 39.6"

THE LEMON DROP WONDER, James Maron's '95 Volvo 850, rattled as it pushed between thirty and thirty-five, trying to merge onto the San Francisco-Oakland Bay Bridge. Despite the assurances of his mechanic, James always worried the transmission or some other vital part of the car would simply shake out the bottom, leaving him stranded on the freeway and tying up traffic for hours.

Luckily, it *was* late Sunday afternoon and the traffic was reasonably light, giving him the longer-than-average time he needed to accelerate up to sixty.

Usually when he and his boyfriend, Gabe Juarez, spent a night out, Gabe picked him up in either his classic Mustang or his new Tesla. But Gabe needed to spend half his Saturday in his office, so they had ended up taking separate cars into the city the night before. Which was why James dared to risk his car on the Bay Bridge on a Sunday afternoon.

He checked his dashboard clock. If he stayed lucky, he could make it home by three thirty and get to the laundromat. He hated doing the wash on Mondays. The place always filled up with people who didn't know how to use the machines and ignored basic laundromat etiquette, like don't leave your wash sitting when there's a line for the machine.

In the distance James saw flashing red-and-blue lights. Behind him, he could hear an ambulance siren approaching. Traffic slowed and ground to a halt.

"Crap."

FOR THE MILLIONTH TIME, a load of baseball gear left by the apartment door nearly sent James tumbling. It was one of the very few things he would not miss when Dylan left for college. He checked his watch and saw it was pushing five in the afternoon. He could technically still make it to the laundromat and get a couple of loads through, but the place filled up quick after five and it became difficult to get the good machines.

Dylan came out of his room, his hair sticking up at odd angles from his postpractice shower. "Hey, Dad. I was starting to worry. How did the concert go last night?"

As a last-second surprise, Gabe had gotten them tickets to the California Honeydrops at the Fillmore. After a couple glasses of wine, Gabe had even talked him into dancing. "It was good. Stop leaving your gear by the door."

"Good?" Dylan tried for a scolding look, but there was too much humor in his eyes. "No, just *good* does not end with you coming home... um... twenty-one hours later than expected."

Dylan had been nagging him about getting a social life and a boyfriend for years, but James hadn't realized he would become so nosy about it once it happened.

You'd think he was the parent here. "The concert ran a bit late, and we got a room in the city." Then they decided not to leave that room until a few hours after the normal checkout time, followed by a late lunch.

"Which hotel?"

"Does it matter?" James asked as he picked up Dylan's baseball gear.

"It might."

"The Saint Francis," James muttered, deciding to risk a Monday wash.

"Again? Well, here's to scoring a sugar daddy."

"What?" James froze for a second as he tucked a baseball bat under his arm.

Dylan headed for the kitchen and rummaged around the fridge. "I mean, a guy with a steady job is a good thing these days, but one who can score you concert tickets and hotel suites on a whim is a pretty sweet deal." He pulled an apple from the veggie bin.

"He's not—"

James felt his phone buzz in his pocket. He juggled around the gear until he could pull it out and saw he had missed a call ten minutes earlier.

"He's not what?"

"Hi. It's me." Gabe's voice had a tinny echo. "Stuck in traffic. Seriously, traffic on a Sunday. I think the Niners are playing or something. Don't worry, I'm on the hands-free setup. Just wanted to say I had a really nice time this weekend. The concert was a lot of fun. The other activities were fun too. Don't know how busy I'm going to be this week, but I'd love to be able to come up there for lunch or dinner. Catch a movie or something. Oh, Tamyra left me nine messages, the last one informing me that I'm getting 'Genie in a Bottle' for my new ringtone. I'm hoping I can pass it off as a postmodern ironic statement or something. Oh look. Traffic is moving. Well, I'll talk to you later. Drive carefully. Bye."

James kept the phone to his ear even after the message ended. Dylan stared at him, one eyebrow raised. He had a funny feeling Dylan practiced that look in the mirror.

James hung up the phone. "You know what? My love life is none of your business."

THE DIM SUM restaurant was decked out in so much red and gold it was almost kitsch. But the food was good, and it wasn't too crowded for a weekday afternoon. The ability to find restaurants that look like they should be average but in truth were excellent seemed to be Gabe's special gift.

James could only assume Gabe used his car as a mobile office a lot. It could be an hour drive from Gabe's office to Berkeley, in good traffic, which was no small amount of time to take out of a Friday afternoon for a lunch date.

His plate had a collection of sticky-bun wrappers and eggroll crumbs. If he kept letting Gabe take him out to eat, he'd go from skinny to flabby pretty quick. He wondered if maybe he should ask Dylan about a workout plan after all. It couldn't hurt to be in better shape.

James was reaching for another sweet pork bun when a phone rang. He looked at Gabe, then around the restaurant before realizing it was his phone. It wasn't showing him any kind of caller ID, but that was a sporadic feature. Actually, ringing qualified as a sporadic feature at times.

He answered it while quickly excusing himself. "Hello?"

"Hello, Mr. Maron?"

"Yes?"

"My name is Vice Principal Robert Jessup. I'm calling about your son, Dylan."

James' heart leapt into his throat and his mind zipped

through an extensive list of worst-case scenarios. "Yes. What's wrong? What happened?"

"I'm sorry to say that Dylan was involved in an altercation not too long ago."

"He what?"

"He was in a fight."

"What?" James knew what he had just heard could not possibly be right, that they must be talking about the wrong child.

"And as I'm sure you're aware, we have a strict code of conduct at this school, especially concerning our athletes, and—"

"This is a mistake. Dylan doesn't fight." James could feel his hand begin to shake. *It has to be a mistake. Has to be. Dylan doesn't fight. Dylan has a clean record. Too much is riding on him having a clean record.*

"I'm sorry, there's been no mistake."

"Look. There has been a mistake and I will be coming there and this will get sorted out!" James hung up the phone and went back to the table.

Gabe stood as he approached. "What's wrong?"

"I have to go. They said Dylan got in a fight. Dylan never fights, but they'll kick him off the team if they think he did, and —" James felt the anger and confusion get replaced with panic.

"Do you need a lift?"

"No," James answered automatically as he gathered his coat. "Shit! Yes. I'm sorry. Dylan has the car today."

"It's not a problem. Come on." Gabe waved to Jared and Tamyra, his driver and PA, who were enjoying their own sticky buns at a separate table. "Let's go rescue Dylan."

THE CEMENT-AND-LINOLEUM HALLS echoed as James rushed to

the school's main office with Gabe and Tamyra in his wake. In the waiting area outside the administrative offices, Dylan sat on a wooden bench, holding an ice pack to his face. On the other side were three large boys—if they could even still be called boys—one with a bloody nose and the other two holding ice packs to sensitive parts of their anatomy.

James sat next to his son and pulled him in for a quick but careful hug. "Are you okay? What happened?"

"I'm fine, Dad, really." Dylan lowered the ice pack. His cheek and eye were bruised and swelling, but it didn't look too bad. He looked up at Gabe. "Hi, Gabe."

"Hey there. Nice bruises."

"Thanks."

James put the ice pack back on Dylan's eye. "Now, what happened? You got in a fight? You don't fight."

"It was sort of a fight."

"Sort of? How do you sort of fight?"

Dylan carefully opened and closed his right hand, which was swelling noticeably. "You know Melinda?"

James tried to run down a depressingly long list of Dylan's girlfriends.

"Lab partner? Chemistry? Quiet, a little frumpy, came around a few times last year?"

"Yes. Right. Lab partner."

"Yeah. Anyway, I was taking a shortcut between classes around the back of the art shed, and those assholes were there, and they had Melinda backed up against the wall. I mean, she carried my ass through chemistry last semester, and she looked scared, and it looked like things were about to get really ugly so —" Dylan waved his hand a little toward the thugs, then his eye.

James felt torn. Dylan getting kicked off the team or suspended from school could screw up so many plans. Everything they worked so hard for could vanish with the stroke of an administrative pen. On the other hand, he'd raised a son willing to take on three thugs to protect someone weaker.

He pulled Dylan in close, more for his own comfort. "We will work this out somehow. I promise."

The door labeled Vice Principal Robert Jessup opened, and a small man in a brown suit poked his head out. He looked at James. "Ah, Mr. Maron. Thank you for coming. A moment of your time?"

James gave Dylan a quick hug.

"Want some backup?" Gabe asked.

"Sure." James had far more serious matters to focus on than questioning why Gabe wanted to join him.

The office was small, with just a desk, filing cabinet, a couple of chairs, and a couch. James sat in the chair across from the desk. Gabe sat on the couch. He stretched his legs out in front of him, crossed them at the ankles, and spread his arms wide, resting them along the top of the couch.

James looked over his shoulder, giving Gabe a look of irritation. He obviously did not appreciate just how serious the situation was, or he would not be taking everything so casually. Gabe just raised his eyebrows, as if asking a question.

James turned back to Mr. Jessup. He could see Dylan's file open and tried to read it upside down.

"Now, Mr. Maron, as I'm sure you know, all our student athletes sign a code of conduct."

"He was trying to defend someone else. It's not like he went looking for or picked a fight." James could feel his cell phone in his pocket and was already considering calling the number he'd had memorized since he was fourteen.

"The fact is that an act of violence takes two people, and there are appropriate ways of handling situations."

"Three against one is a little more than two people."

"Be that as it may, the school still has policies and procedures in place—"

"Bob," Gabe suddenly cut in, and James whipped around. "Can I call you Bob? From where I'm sitting, Bob, what we have here is actually a very simple situation." Gabe hadn't moved from his casual sprawl. "What we have is a young man —a baseball star with classic all-American looks and a spotless record, raised by a single father in difficult conditions, now heading to Stanford on a scholarship—who saw a poor, shy, bullied girl beset upon by *three* nearly grown men. And knowing full well that he was outnumbered and his actions could—and most likely would—lead to severe personal injury, he still put himself willingly at risk to defend this lone student and stop what could have become the worst kind of crime."

"Who are you?" Mr. Jessup asked.

"Now I'm sure you've been threatened by lawyers before," Gabe continued, ignoring the question. "This is California—'I'll see you in court' is practically a greeting. But you see, there are far, far worse people than lawyers in the world. There are public relations specialists. And I'm not talking about the kind who put out press releases and spin gaffes. I'm talking about the kind who are hired by presidential candidates and paid in cash out of nondisclosed campaign slush funds. The things they could do with a simple little story like this...." Gabe shook his head a little. He brought his arms forward, steepled his fingers, and peered over them.

"Who are you?" Mr. Jessup asked again, a slight stutter in his words.

"Now, this suit I'm wearing cost twenty-five hundred euros. I bought two others at the same time during a conference in Venice. If I'm willing to drop that kind of cash on a whim, what do you think I'd be willing to spend protecting a kid I'm actually reasonably fond of?" Gabe peered at Bob for about five seconds, never blinking, the tiniest smile on his face.

Mr. Jessup sputtered a bit and James reeled, his heart pounding.

Gabe leaned forward ever so slowly. "Come on, Bob, do the right thing."

Before Mr. Jessup had a chance to answer, there was a tap at the door and Tamyra poked her head in. "So sorry to interrupt." She held out a cell phone to Gabe. "You *really* need to take this, and I moved your two thirty to four thirty and your four thirty to seven tomorrow morning, but he's not happy about it."

"Is he ever happy?" Gabe grabbed the phone and quickly stepped from the office, mouthing a quick "Sorry" to James.

Bob turned to James, looking distinctly rattled. James felt rattled himself. He'd never seen Gabe like that. Every casual-seeming move Gabe had just made must have been coldly deliberate. Was that how he acted in business negotiations? Or during a fight? Was that how Gabe fought?

"Who was that?" Bob asked one more time.

"Um… my boyfriend?"

Bob looked down at Dylan's record and swallowed a few times. "Well, seeing as how Dylan's never been in real trouble, if he's willing to spend Saturday washing off some graffiti, sit through the standard conflict resolution lecture, and this doesn't become a habit, then I don't see why we'd need to make any more of this, really."

"Thank you." James didn't let the staggering relief show on his face. Instead, he smiled politely. "Dylan will be glad to hear that, and I'll be sure to talk to him myself." James stood. "Do call me if there are any other problems."

"Absolutely."

James nodded and let himself out.

Dylan jumped up from the bench as soon as he saw James. "Dad?"

"It's fine. You'll need to scrub some graffiti and just don't make a habit of it."

Dylan did let the relief show on his face as he let out a deep breath and pulled James into a quick one-armed hug. "No problem."

"How's your eye?"

Dylan lowered the ice pack, giving James a second look. It was going to turn solidly black and blue, he could tell already. "I've taken worse from a pop fly. Coach Frasier is still going to yell."

James inspected the slight abrasions on Dylan's knuckles. "Are your hands okay?"

Dylan smiled. "I'm fine, Dad, really."

"Your ankle?" James asked. There was always a risk that it could go out from an old injury, which could damage his scholarship almost as badly as getting suspended.

"It's fine. I'm fine. I swear."

Mr. Jessup poked his head out of his office and motioned to Dylan. "Moment of your time as well?"

"I'll see you tonight?" James asked. He knew Dylan had no plans for dates or practice that night, but he still needed to hear it.

"I'll be there." Dylan gave James another tight hug. "Thanks," he whispered.

James just gave him a hug back before Dylan grabbed his bag, gave Gabe a smile and a nod, then went to talk to the vice principal himself. James turned to Gabe. He was looking at his phone but had a smile on his face. The fear and slight adrenaline dropped out of his system, replaced by anger.

"I could have handled that."

Gabe looked up. "What?"

"Dylan's had personality clashes with teachers and some administrators. I've talked him out of trouble before."

"Sorry, I just thought—"

"I can take care of my own son." James could not count how many times he'd said those words to people who thought they were helping or were under the impression that James needed help. "Coach Frasier would have had our back, and if all else failed, I could have called Sanderson."

"Who?"

"Steven Sanderson, our lawyer. He did Dylan's custody pro bono."

"Is he the guy who has those really sleazy commercials on at like two in the morning, with that annoying jingle? 'If you're gonna sue, sue with Sanderson'?"

"Yes, and he's a very good lawyer." James was always willing to defend Sanderson despite the sleazy commercials and incredibly irritating jingle. "And he probably wouldn't have been needed anyway, and—"

Gabe put his hands up slightly. "Sorry, I just thought I could help expedite things for you."

James felt a slight ache in his jaw from clenching his teeth. "Do you really know those kinds of PR people?"

Gabe barked with laughter. "God, no. I don't even know if those people exist. I mean, I'm sure they do, but we don't use them."

James relaxed a little. It was nice to know his boyfriend didn't associate with those kinds of people, but at the same time, he hated to think what might have happened if the vice principal had called Gabe's bluff.

Tamyra touched Gabe's shoulder. "Sorry, but I really need to get you going."

"That's what she said," Gabe muttered quietly.

Tamyra rolled her eyes, and they quickly moved down the echoing, tiled halls, James following.

James looked over Gabe's suit from the corner of his eye. It was a very nice suit, but still just a suit. "Did you really spend twenty-five hundred euros on that suit?"

Gabe's look became a little shifty. "I occasionally indulge in retail therapy. I got dumped via text for a barista slash unpublished poet."

The idea of spending what amounted to several months of James' pay on clothes simply wouldn't compute. The closest he'd ever come to retail therapy was a Freight and Salvage's open mic night, and that came to all of eight dollars.

The rich really did live in a completely different world.

———

THE MACARONI and cheese bubbled as James pulled it out of the oven. It wasn't exactly the healthiest meal—or the cheapest when made with real cheese—but it was first-class comfort food, and James thought he and Dylan could use a bit.

The heat had started to bite through the thin hot pads when he heard Dylan come in. "Dylan!" he called out as he quickly placed the mac and cheese on the table, his fingers starting to burn.

Dylan came in, following his nose. "Oh, that smells nice."

"Thought we could both use it."

James looked Dylan over. The bruise started at his eye and went all the way down his cheek. He could easily see the outline of a fist, and it was going to be impressive by the next morning. His right hand had swelled slightly, but thankfully he didn't have a game that weekend.

James had spent the rest of the day trying to think about what happened from every possible angle. And in between the tangle of emotions, he managed to come to one solid conclusion.

He put his hands on Dylan's shoulders. "Dylan, I want you to know that I'm proud of you."

"Dad—"

"No, I'm serious. You put yourself in danger to stop something that you knew was wrong. It says a lot about your character as a young man. And I am proud of you."

Dylan dipped his head. "I had a good example."

James lowered his head as well. "Okay, enough mushy stuff. Get some plates."

Dylan went to the counter and pulled a couple of plates from the drying rack by the sink. "So, I heard from Mrs. Anders, the secretary, that Gabe completely trampled Mr. Jessup, scared the shit right out of him."

James cleared his throat a bit. He did not need to get a reputation for hardball tactics or relying on a rich boyfriend to get Dylan out of trouble for something James could have managed on his own.

"Well, he does make a living negotiating things."

"No shit. Hey, I don't suppose you know anything more about that Russian deal he's working on?"

"No." James tried not to snap, but it still came out a bit hard. "And if I did, I'm sure he wouldn't want me spreading it around to gossipy teenagers."

Dylan raised his hands in quick surrender. "No problem. I will try not to let my serious curiosity get in the way of your good time."

"Thank you."

James' phone bleeped. He was pretty sure he had it set to chirp when a text came in, but randomly shifting ringtones was one of the more interesting "features" of his awful phone.

Hi. Sorry for butting in earlier. Hope Dylan's OK. Dinner next Friday? Know a good Thai place.

"Gabe?"

"Yeah, he's just checking in."

"Attentive boyfriends are good things. As I've had several girlfriends tell me."

An unpleasant feeling reemerged at Dylan's words.

Dylan's fine. Free next Friday.

James didn't look up from his phone. "Just eat your dinner."

2

The air was cool but dry, and a little cleaner from the afternoon fog rolling out. Gabe took a couple of deep breaths as he got out of his car. He'd texted James often over the previous few days, but a weird vibe still floated between them. James' replies were friendly but shorter than usual. It also seemed to take him longer to respond, but that could just be his phone. Gabe hoped it was nothing but irrational relationship panic on his end, that he was reading too much into signs that weren't there and meant nothing. James could be going through a busy stint at work. Or maybe he was still stressed over Dylan's fight.

He punched the code on the security gate and climbed the stairs, the elevator still bearing an out-of-order sign. Cracked and yellowed tape held the sign in place. The rough base threads of the carpet on the first step were clearly visible through the wear. He knocked on James' door, bouncing on his toes with atypical nerves.

The door opened, and Dylan quickly ushered him in. "Dad's not home yet. I got a message from him, and he was just leaving work. Apparently it was one of those 'everybody spends all day being really demanding, then everything breaks at the last minute' days."

"I know all about those."

Dylan's phone began to ring. He checked the number, then moved quickly to the hall. Gabe wondered if it was yet another girlfriend. James often complained about his complete inability to keep track of Dylan's relationships at any given point.

Gabe looked around the living room. He had never spent any time alone in it. He'd learned long ago that you could tell a lot about a person by what books they kept. The mix, placed neatly on plywood and brick shelves, was reasonably eclectic. Some popular science books, several heavy coffee-table art books with sun-faded covers, despite the lack of windows, and battered copies of *Alice's Adventures in Wonderland* and *The Lord of the Rings*. Well-read collections of Steinbeck and Hemingway. A row of cheap-looking paperbacks with titles like *El corazón de la rosa* and *Enamorarse antes del amanecer* dominated an upper shelf. Gabe took down a couple. The cover art looked like it belonged to a bad romance novel. The blurbs on the back sounded like telenovelas with tragic love, secret children, and conniving land barons. On the lowest shelf was a stack of thick spiral-bound notebooks. He took one off the top and flipped it open, finding the word "Budget."

In James' tidy handwriting was a monthly budget, and judging by the date it was almost five years old. The top number must have been his monthly pay. It wasn't much. Gabe made in a few hours what James made in a month. The first expense listed was "Savings." It took nearly half of the check. He flipped forward a few pages. Savings seemed to claim half or more of every check.

After that the lists showed utility bills, grocery, gas, laundry, bus pass, phone, then another small input number listed as "rollover." It seemed to be what little, if anything, remained from the previous month. He flipped through pages, watching the months go by. At some point James got a raise, but all that seemed to mean was that more went into the savings. Though after the raise, there were new items added to the list, like physical therapy. Not cheap.

Gabe hadn't gotten to be CFO on just his looks. He'd always had the ability to process large quantities of numbers in his head quite quickly and keep track of multiple sets of them, so within a minute, he had a pretty clear view of James' finances.

Dylan had been right. They could afford to live a *little* better. Maybe get a slightly less terrifying car, but the fact that savings was the first item on the budget list said a lot. Of course, according to Gabe's calculations, even putting aside as much as they could every month, the savings would still be modest at best. As he flipped through, he noticed a pattern under the "Rollover" number. There were things like Freight-$8, Haircut-$10, Shoes (Dylan)-$30. As he got toward more recent months, the rollover amount started shrinking. The month of their first date had the line Freight (2)-$16. Then Extra Gas-$53, New Shirt-$5. Gabe once had a boyfriend, in a fit of pique, ask him how much a relationship was worth. He could now tell him to damn near the cent. He felt guilty and made a note to come up more often instead of having James come down to him. Especially with gas prices already bad and getting steadily higher.

He flipped back and forth between months. Something felt wrong about the budgets. The math kept adding up fine until he realized where he'd last seen a budget that looked like the ones in front of him: high school. Everyone had to take a life skills class, where they learned basic home ec, why they shouldn't do drugs, got a first aid lecture, and at least one assignment was working out a monthly budget. They'd been given numbers and had to work out how to live within their constraints. Gabe had gotten an A, but the fact was that he'd never seen an *adult* write out a functioning budget like that. It was just an exercise. But in front of him were a lifetime of those exercises. Not adult budgets, but the way you write a budget when a teacher is standing over your shoulder. Careful, precise, and every penny under managed control. But James was managing it somehow, living exactly within his means and still saving everything he could. It was impressive in its way. It spoke to a lifestyle most people couldn't or wouldn't manage. It was something to be proud of.

Gabe heard keys at the door. He put the notebook back on the pile and grabbed up the yearbook Dylan had once shown him. James stumbled in, his posture one of exhaustion, but a smile flicked across his face as soon as he saw Gabe.

Gabe flipped the yearbook back open to page forty-seven. "They let you bring Dylan to school?"

James dropped his bag. "Once a quarter for health education. I was told no amount of safe sex talks can compare to the sound of a wailing infant or toddler's temper tantrum echoing down the halls. Had a bunch of jocks get mad at me because all the girls in school started refusing to put out."

Dylan came out of the hall. "Hi, Dad, my ride is here." He gave his father a kiss on the cheek. "Bye, Dad." And he was out the door.

James watched his son leave, then took the yearbook from Gabe and looked at the picture. "I can't remember half of this. It's basically a three-year blur. I mainly remember being tired."

Gabe took the book away and placed it back on the shelf. He wanted to gather James up in his arms and just hold him. "Speaking of tired."

"I'm fine." James quickly smiled, but it was obviously forced. "Really."

Gabe gently rubbed his thumb along the back of James' neck. His head fell forward, and he started moaning. Gabe rubbed a little harder, and James slowly leaned forward until his forehead pressed against Gabe's shoulder. Gabe felt himself begin to relax as well.

"Why don't we skip going out? Let's stay in, and I'll give you a backrub."

James let out a long breath. "I'd argue and say I'm fine to go out, but I spent half the day squeezing myself under desks and the other half running from one end of campus to the other and back again, mainly doing other people's jobs on top of my own, and your hand feels really nice doing that."

Gabe stopped rubbing James' neck before tilting James' head up and giving him a soft kiss. "Why don't we find some place where you can lay down."

"Are you sure? I mean, if you want to go out…?" James waved toward the door.

Gabe shook his head. His own week had seemed to drag with a never-ending swarm of little prickly problems filling all his time. "It's fine. Come on. Let's get you relaxed."

James kissed him back, then dragged himself down the hall. Gabe followed. The walls of James' bedroom were a faded pale yellow and nearly bare except for two framed photos, one of an infant and one of a little blond boy, about four. A chest of drawers was along one wall. A bedside table with a few paperbacks on it and a bed was against another wall. The bed made Gabe want to cry. Obviously meant for one, it even looked a little short to be a full-size adult bed. It would be nearly impossible to get a second person into it. He wouldn't be the slightest bit surprised if he found out it was James' childhood bed, never upgraded because the idea of putting anyone else into it was so far away. James sat on the edge of his bed.

"You do look tired."

James rubbed at his eyes. "Sorry, just been a long week."

"Why don't you get undressed, and we'll see if that week can end on a better note."

James smiled and began to undress. Gabe saw him wince as he pulled his shirt over his head. "Lay down. Let me see that cute backside of yours."

James half chuckled and shook his head, but he did lay down. Gabe was right. Less than a foot remained between James' feet and the end of the bed. He wondered if he should even risk getting up on it, if it would support both their weight. Of course, if the bed did break, he'd have a valid excuse to get James a new one.

He stripped off his own clothes, down to his shorts since naked back rubs were always better, then climbed onto the bed, straddling James' backside. The springs creaked, and the mattress sagged, but the bed held up. Gabe took a few preliminary swipes, wishing he had some oil, then pressed his thumbs into James' neck right at the base of his skull.

"Oh my God," James slurred into his pillow.

Gabe smiled to himself and kept on going. He'd picked up a trick or two from various partners over the years and had his personal technique down pretty well. He worked his way slowly down James' neck, enjoying the constant moans of pleasure. Sometimes he would hit a spot and James' body would jolt under him. He'd work those spots gently until the muscles under them stopped twitching.

He had only made it to James' shoulders when he reached full hardness. Straddled over James' ass, his body desperately wanted to strip off those last few pieces of fabric, to slide into James and make him moan with pleasure. He firmly told his body not to get its hopes up. At least not as far as that night went.

He went for a softer touch as he got to James' upper back,

avoiding some hard-angled bruises, most likely from the underside of desks. Every muscle was tight, and there were knots upon knots. He decided that James' birthday present, or whatever legitimate excuse he could think of to get James a present, would be a professional massage. Or better yet, a day-spa trip for the both of them. It would have to be sometime after the madness with the Russians eased up, though. His spine felt like it needed a professional realignment as much as the Lemon Drop Wonder did.

James' moans quieted into heavy breaths as Gabe carefully worked the heels of his hands into the flesh around James' shoulder blades. As he did that, he let his mind wander. It flitted to work first, which it always did, but he brushed that out of his way as best as he could. He steered his mind toward James again. The first thought there was sex, but he brushed that away as well. He thought about how he'd talk James into a spa day. It wouldn't be James' "kind of thing." It hadn't been Gabe's "kind of thing" either. He had once disdained rich twits who could afford to have mud masks while people rubbed their feet, but the foot rubs were close to orgasmic at this one place he knew up in Napa.

He wondered if he could give it to James for Dylan's upcoming eighteenth birthday. A sort of "Congratulations, you raised your kid to adulthood, now let yourself relax for two hours" gift. He might even get James away for an entire weekend on that one. He'd say he didn't need it, but if Gabe could talk a bunch of Russians out of billions of dollars of mineral rights, then he should be able to tempt James away from his monastic lifestyle for a day or two. Of course, why stop with a spa—how about a trip to Paris on the company jet? For all Gabe had done, he'd never made the mile-high club. And what exactly was the point of working hard to get filthy rich if you couldn't spoil your boyfriend from time to time? Your boyfriend who claimed he didn't want things.

Gabe shook his head in disbelief. Years of men perfectly happy to take the luxury lifestyle he offered, until they realized Gabe's work schedule came with it, and he finally fell for one whose idea of an indulgence was an eight-dollar concert ticket a few times a year, and always seemed perfectly okay to let him deal with work.

He'd worked his way down to James' midback when James let out a small moan before his breathing slid into the slow and steady rhythm of sleep. He was sure James needed it. Gabe eased up but didn't fully stop. He knelt there, his legs going slightly numb, stroking James' back, letting himself enjoy the sensation of another's warm, smooth skin. James mumbled and shifted slightly. Gabe climbed off, shaking the pins and needles out of his feet as James rolled onto his side, still half asleep. He took it as an invitation.

He eased himself onto the sliver of bed, listening to the springs squeak and groan as he shifted around. He pulled James into his arms, partly to anchor himself. James mumbled again, then went right back to sleep.

THE HEAVY FOG of sleep was still ghosting around James' mind, trying to lure him back down, when he opened his eyes to find that he was nose to nose with Gabe. He seemed to do that a lot around Gabe, just doze off. He had thought that it was because of Gabe's stupidly comfortable bed, but now it seemed it might simply be Gabe. Or it might have been the ten miles he'd put on his feet that day.

Gabe opened his eyes as well. "Hi," he whispered.

"I fell asleep again," James said by way of apology.

"I don't mind."

"You should. It's not like this is a short trip for you."

Gabe brushed his fingers across his face. "I don't mind. I'll take all the time with you I can get. Even if you're asleep. Time with you is time I'm not at work. I almost feel like I'm having a torrid affair. Cheating on TechPrim with you."

"You shouldn't neglect anything that's important," James said without a thought.

"It's all important, and I don't." Gabe kissed him. He tasted like sweet coffee. Gabe rolled against him slowly. It didn't feel sexual. More like sitting on the beach and letting the waves roll over your legs while the sun went down. Gabe's lips slipped from his, and he pulled back. He looked into Gabe's soft brown eyes. They seemed tired, and maybe even a hair sad, but James felt something change. Something in his head suddenly slid to the side and locked in with something else. Something in his chest squeezed and twisted in an odd way.

Gabe's fingers trailed across James' face, brushing aside a stray wisp of hair. James had plans for a haircut but hadn't found the time. Gabe kissed him again, and James let himself go. It was all so easy to do around Gabe, just take his hands off the wheel. But that was how people crashed and burned. He kissed back and tried to press himself closer. Gabe suddenly grabbed onto him tight and let out a scared little squeak as he started to slide off the bed. James quickly scooted as close to the wall as he could get, pulling Gabe a few inches closer onto the bed.

"Let me guess, you've had this bed since you were ten?"

"Fourteen. Dylan used it too, but he got too tall."

Gabe nodded and gave him a gentle kiss.

That funny squeeze was back, but it felt almost painful this time. He'd never thought about his bed before. Never thought about putting anyone else in it. It was a bed. It kept his body off the floor while he slept. He should get a new one, that was obvious, a larger one, but it was easier to ignore the fact that there was only one person in his bed when it barely fit him. He squeezed his eyes shut. Gabe kissed them.

"What's wrong?" Gabe whispered.

"Nothing," James whispered back. The lie must have been obvious, and he could only hope Gabe would ignore it. The more time he spent with Gabe, the harder it was to ignore all the things that were wrong with his life. All the places he'd never gone. Experiences he'd never had. All the wants buried deep and regularly beaten back down, and the knowledge that Gabe could give him so much of what he wanted. And what could Gabe possibly want in return? It was something James still hadn't worked out. He had marginal skills in bed. His looks were the very definition of average. He thought that maybe Gabe was just looking for a distraction from his job, but that couldn't last long. And what would all that leave him with? A bed too big for one.

Gabe squeezed him tight. "What's wrong?" he asked again.

"Just a lot of stuff on my mind."

"Anything I can do to help?"

James' mind screamed, *Yes!* "No. I'm fine. Just a little tired. I'm used to it."

Gabe kissed him again. "I can't imagine how tired you must be."

"I'm sure you're juggling a million more things than I am." Gabe's phone started buzzing. He didn't move. "You should get that."

"No. I shouldn't."

James frowned. Work was not something he could ever afford to ignore. He didn't like to think that Gabe was letting work slide to be with him. "Could be important."

Gabe brushed a thumb across his cheek. "This is important."

James squeezed his eyes shut again. It was becoming hard to breathe. He wondered if this was what the start of a heart attack felt like. One of those freak ones that drops healthy people in their thirties. His parents could take care of Dylan, he thought. He didn't have a large life insurance policy, but he didn't have debts either. Chris, the most senior of his team, knew where he kept the admin passwords and could be bumped into his job temporarily. Funerals cost a lot; cremations were cheaper.

Suddenly Gabe's lips were on his, hard and forceful. His tongue demanded entrance. His body enveloped James', rolling him over, pressing down on him, hands in his hair pulling almost too tight. James didn't try to resist, unable to do anything but submit to Gabe's force of body and will washing over him.

Just as suddenly, Gabe pulled back. James opened his eyes and sucked in deep gulps of air, his heart racing.

"Sorry, but you looked on the verge of a panic attack. I don't know why, but I'm sure it's something that can be managed."

"I…," James stuttered and took a few breaths. He ran over his mental map of the server room cabling in his head. It was mostly logical, devoid of emotion, and complicated enough to push little fluttery, half-formed, unpleasant thoughts out of his head. He took another deep breath. "It was nothing."

"No. It was something."

"It was… sometimes things… sometimes I realize I don't have a proper plan for certain eventualities. And it bothers me a bit." Gabe frowned. "Please don't look at me like that," James nearly begged.

"Like what?"

"Pity."

"Never. You're too strong. I just worry about you."

"You shouldn't." James could worry about himself; no one needed to do that for him.

"I'm your boyfriend. I'm allowed to worry about you. It's one of the perks."

"Perks? One more thing to worry about."

"One more thing I *want* to worry about and make time for.

Now what was the eventuality you didn't have a plan for? Planning is something I'm very good at."

"I don't want to talk about it." James felt a hard, burning knot settle into his throat. "It's nothing. I'm sorry. I think I'm more tired than I realized."

"Do you want me to go?"

"No," James said quickly. The phone had finally stopped buzzing, but that didn't mean the caller didn't leave a message Gabe should be attending to. "Unless you have somewhere you need to be. I mean, if I'm keeping you from something important...."

Gabe kissed him hard again, then pulled back. "I told you, this is important."

"It's just—" James couldn't even begin to voice it. His throat grew tight again, and the words tangled in his head. He took a deep breath, his lungs filling with Gabe's scent. He felt small tremors run through his body. They'd happened before and far too often. It was a prelude to panic or tears. To something he couldn't control but could usually hide away from anyone's notice. At least when another person wasn't nose to nose with him.

"What is it?" Gabe asked again, and James was sure he would keep asking.

"If something happens to me, could you keep an eye on Dylan for a little bit?"

"What! What's wrong? Nothing's going to happen to you."

"I... I know, I just don't handle things I can't—" James shook his head as if he could simply brush away the thoughts. It was a stupid thing to say. Now Gabe was going to get a real idea of how messed up he was and how much his holding it together was an act. "I'm sorry." James' eyes were still closed. The inside of his head was beginning to feel ragged, and even though it was mostly because of Gabe, he felt more grounded with Gabe holding him.

Gabe kissed him softly. "I understand. Of course I will. And nothing is going to happen." Gabe kissed him again.

James' chest still hurt. "Gabe, I have a funny feeling that I might be a little messed up." It was the first time he'd admitted it out loud to anyone.

"No. You're not. You're tired and stressed, and you have been for a while. Just like me."

"Are you sure?"

"I'm sure. I've seen messed up. I've dated messed up. Messed up is having panic attacks over the feng shui of your apartment until you OD on Valium, then dump your boyfriend halfway through the rehab he's paying for."

James chuckled, the knot in his chest beginning to ease. "I keep panicking over little things. Anything I can't predict. The closer it gets to Dylan leaving, the more terrified I get over the little stupid things, and I know he's grown up, and I know I need to start letting go and living my life, but I swear he started kindergarten yesterday, and it's just...."

"It's hard."

"Yeah. It really is. And what am I supposed to do in September?" James asked, mostly to himself. "I am thirty-two. What am I supposed to do with the rest of my existence?"

"I don't know. Live it, I guess."

James wanted to laugh at that, even though there was nothing funny about it.

"But for just a weekend of it, I was thinking, after Dylan's graduation, and once I've got a break from the Russians, we could maybe drive down the coast? I know a little bed-and-breakfast in Monterey run by a nice couple. We could go to the aquarium. Maybe rent one of those kayaks, paddle out and look at the sea otters?" There was a cautiously hopeful look on Gabe's face.

James thought that it did sound nice, the idea of sitting by the water, listening to waves, not thinking about things. It would cost, though. Everything cost in some way in the end: money, time, something.

"I… I'd have to look at my leave schedule."

"Okay." Gabe shifted around until they were both on their sides again, pressed chest to chest. "I have a feeling that by then we'll both be wanting a weekend someplace quiet."

James nodded. "Can we stay like this for a while, now?"

"Of course."

He pressed his face to Gabe's chest and fought the urge to fall back asleep. He'd been worried about seeing Gabe after their last aborted lunch. There had been an odd tension to the texts and phone calls, but as soon as Gabe had touched his neck and he had felt the warmth of his fingers and the strength in his hands, he could think of little else. He had been told often that he shouldn't get angry at people who tried to help, but most of the time, he didn't need help. People didn't understand that. Gabe had just assumed. James took a deep breath, drawing in Gabe's scent before he could get angry again at something that was past.

Gabe kept asking him what he wanted. What he wanted were Gabe's hands on his body at every possible moment. Not necessarily sexual touches, though those were nice, but the simple feeling of skin on his skin was becoming something he craved.

He tried to pull those thoughts in. They were dangerous but fast becoming hard to ignore. Gabe stroked his head, and he gritted his teeth. He usually came home from bad days and shoved his nose in a book. Maybe went to bed early. He took care of the anger quietly and without witnesses, like so much else in his life. He wondered if this was what being in a relationship really was about: having to endure someone watching your breakdowns and neuroses and witnessing the days when you just want to shove a towel in your mouth, scream, then go to bed.

Gabe went from stroking his head to rubbing it gently. James felt his own body melt against the bed. Gabe started making little nonsense hushing noises. He tried to lift his arms, but he felt weak and heavy, and he didn't seem to care. Finally he took a deep breath and drifted off again.

GABE STROKED JAMES' head long past the point he had drifted back to sleep, leaving him with his own thoughts. James' near panic attack had been a greater shock than he'd let show. The whole night was throwing him for a loop. He could simply chalk it up to the chronic exhaustion James was certainly dealing with. It was a state he was familiar with, and he was well aware that it could send the brain tumbling quickly into weird dark places. But the cracks Gabe had just seen, had been allowed to see, seemed to go deeper than simple exhaustion. They seemed to go right down to James' heart, where they would be hard to fix.

But Gabe was a fixer. Companies, people, it didn't matter. There was nothing that couldn't be dealt with once the core problem was determined. In James' case at least one major problem was easy to work out. He was poor, and like a billion other people, he was stuck in a loop. And it wasn't as if he'd screwed up to get there. He didn't overleverage himself on a million-dollar mortgage. He didn't lose his job with fifty grand sitting on credit cards. He didn't go through some ugly divorce. He started at the bottom of the ladder and did his level best to claw his way up with what he had.

Gabe sighed and let himself roll some fantasies around in his head. James moving in with him, quitting his shitty job, going back to school to become… something. He wondered what James had wanted to be when he grew up, before everything changed. He wondered if he'd even had a chance to develop a solid idea. His mind jumped to the future. Dylan could come home on the weekends to nice family dinners and lively conversation.

Gabe closed his eyes. It had been a long time since he'd fantasized about playing happy family with anyone and even longer since he felt even a hint of seriousness in that.

He heard his phone go off. James stirred. He wanted to pick up his phone, fling it across the room, and watch it shatter. He kept stroking James' head, trying to ease him into a deeper sleep, since Gabe still needed time to think. All these little wants and fears and fantasies were adding up to something he hadn't felt in a long time. Something that had gone so unbelievably bad the last time.

With James it would be different, of course. James wasn't a wannabe corporate raider with advanced degrees in psychological manipulation, for one. That was working on the very risky assumption that James had long-term interest in him too. If he was James, he'd want to play the field, at least a little. See who else was out there. Catch up on all the social experiences he'd missed by having Dylan so young. Gabe let out another sigh and shoved those feelings down. At this point, sticking his heart on a platter would probably only lead to James running into the hills and Dylan kicking his ass.

Best to start things slow. Chinese deliveries. Low-key but still nice dates. Buttering up Dylan a bit. Dealing with the Russians so he could take a few days off properly where perhaps they could catch up on sleep together. Not much of a game plan really, but it was a start.

WHEN JAMES finally woke from his second nap, they ordered Chinese food, sat on the couch, and talked about nothing important. They made out on the couch, ate dinner, made out some more, then moved to the bedroom for some precarious lovemaking. It had been after midnight, and James had been fast asleep again when Gabe let himself quietly out of the apartment. He'd left a note by the bed, promising to call.

Now Gabe was using his sliver of a lunch break to query the almighty Internet on dating people with kids. Dylan had mostly come around to his side after he did his best to prove he wasn't screwing with James, but if Gabe wanted to get James out of town, he was going to need Dylan's backing. And any serious relationship moves would quite possibly need Dylan's approval, or at least his advice. Gabe glared at his computer monitor. The all-knowingness of the Internet was failing him. He'd found plenty on step-parenting and a couple of blog posts about dating people with small children, but nothing that seemed to apply to his situation.

Tamyra came in and put a suspiciously healthy-looking sandwich on his desk before plopping herself down on the couch and tucking into a salad of her own.

"Tam, have you ever dated anyone with kids?"

"No. I'm not really good with kids."

Gabe lifted the top piece of whole grain and seed bread on his sandwich and squinted at the sprouts under it. "Me neither."

"My niece was about five when my sister started dating again. Seriously, though, James' kid is practically an adult."

Gabe shoved the sprouts aside to find dandelion greens. "I know. I just want to keep in his good books, and I don't want James to feel like he's losing time with Dylan to be with me."

Tamyra shrugged. "My sister used to do these family dates every month or so with her, Julia, and her boyfriend. They'd go to the zoo. Stuff like that." Gabe pushed aside the dandelion leaves to reveal grilled vegetables. "Stop playing with your sandwich and eat it."

"Only if I find bacon on the bottom."

"You have a meeting in fifteen minutes and you don't have a free second between then and seven. Eat it."

Gabe started chewing on the top slice of bread. "Why are you still my PA?" It was a question he asked himself regularly but only actually asked Tamyra a few times. He'd yet to get a good answer.

"Because you'd die without me."

Gabe pushed aside the rest of his sandwich. He'd swing through marketing later. They always had good leftovers from some department party or networking lunch. "I'm serious. You were supposed to be in the job, what, a year? You have more degrees than I do. You know the fine minutiae of every deal we make. Anyone else would have quit or demanded a transfer after six months of putting up with me. You've never even asked for a raise."

"And yet you give them to me."

"Seriously. What are you doing here?"

Tamyra set aside her salad, which looked about as appetizing as Gabe's sandwich. "Do you remember the state you were in when I started working for you?"

No, Gabe thought. "Vaguely," he answered.

"Exactly. You'd had six PAs in five months. They were all either trying to get into your pants or were praying for your soul. My first day you'd had about three hours of sleep in three days. You were trying to shift around the budget so dependents of employees got free flu shots, in the middle of a bidding war for a half-dozen patents, you were fighting with Frank and Nate over if you should even be trying for the patents, and then a bunch of school kids were dragged in, and you were supposed to give them some sort of inspirational talk."

"Was I inspirational?" Gabe had not a single memory of that day.

"No. You mumbled, babbled, threw in some analogies that made no sense whatsoever, and forgot the name of your own company. The impressive bit was that you pulled yourself up there in that state when any other executive would have just pawned the whole thing off onto someone further down the ladder. I figured at that point you needed someone who wouldn't try to get into your pants, knew your soul was just fine, and would knock you on the back of the head with a two-by-four if that's what was needed for you to get some sleep."

"I wish I could argue with any of that."

"You're good at your job, you run a good business, you're good to your people, but you are crap at taking care of yourself. I'll move on when I find someone who can take care of you half as well as I can."

"Or I shove you out the door."

Tamyra laughed. "Like that's ever going to happen."

―――――

JAMES bent backward and listened to his spine crack. Despite the noises, his back was in better condition, or at least a few decades younger, than Mrs. Gonzales's, which was why he was helping her lug bolts of fabric up the stairs. It was her second granddaughter's quinceañera in a couple of months, and she was sewing all the dresses, which meant stitching up about a million miles of pink satin and tulle.

At least Mrs. Gonzales's granddaughter was shorter than he was. With Mrs. Maldonado's granddaughter's prom dress the previous year, he'd been roped into acting as a living dress stand while it was hemmed, instead of just helping with the hemming. Dylan still had the photos hidden somewhere. He didn't actually mind helping out with things like hauling groceries, rolling tamales, or handstitching a million seed pearls onto white taffeta. The women of the building had acted as Dylan's aunties and grandmothers over the years, providing babysitting, hand-me-downs, advice, and more than a few meals when he and Dylan got truly desperate.

Mrs. Gonzales let them into her apartment where the Virgen de Guadalupe stared at him from at least three walls.

"¿Dónde los quieres?"

"Con los demás."

James put the bolts of fabric on the table with a half dozen others while Mrs. Gonzales went into her kitchen to make them both some coffee.

He followed her into the kitchen, which was identical to his, where she poured them both thick black coffee, then stirred in condensed milk until it was nearly white. "James, I've been seeing you with a man lately? The women are saying you have a boyfriend?"

He accepted a cup of coffee. "I might." He supposed it had to happen sooner or later. Every other person had been the center of gossip in the building at one point or another. James had managed to avoid it, mainly by being the most boring person on earth.

"You might? I think you do. He looks handsome."

James pretended to think about it. "I guess. If you like that type."

"And he looks rich?"

James blew on his coffee. Mrs. Gonzales always made it nuclear hot. "He might be, a little."

"Rich is good."

"It's not important."

"Rich is good. Rich can take care of you and Dylan."

James rolled his eyes. "I don't need anyone taking care of me. I'm not looking for anyone to take care of me. And I take care of Dylan just fine."

Mrs. Gonzales patted the air in front of James. "Of course you do, but it's good to have help. If someone wants to take care of you, you should let them. If they're also kind, and handsome…?"

James sipped his coffee, having no desire to respond to that comment.

"What's his name?"

"Gabe. Gabriel. Juarez." He figured the best thing to do with gossip was to feed it as much detail as possible. It seemed to burn out quicker once there was less to speculate on.

"And where's he from?"

"He grew up in the Bay."

"Have you met his family yet?"

That was something that hadn't been brought up except for a quick mention of his sisters. He'd heard more about Gabe's godchildren. "No, no I haven't."

Mrs. Gonzales gave a slightly disapproving squint. "Make sure he does that soon. A man who is ashamed of his family is not a man you should be associating with."

"I will keep that in mind."

"Good. Now, what does he do? He better have a good job. Rich without work is begging the devil for trouble."

James took a deep breath. He was surprised Dylan hadn't blabbed it around the building. He was as bad a gossip as the rest of them. "He's the chief financial officer of TechPrim Industries." He got a slightly questioning look. James pulled his phone from his pocket and showed her the logo on the back. "TechPrim."

Her eyebrows went up. "He better be taking care of you, then."

"I don't need to be taken care of." James tried not to raise his voice. "I am not a child. I have a job. I manage."

"Doesn't mean you should turn him away if he offers. It can be nice to have someone who wants to be helpful."

"Fine." He didn't want to start a fight.

"And if he causes you trouble, you send him to me."

James stuffed down a laugh. Facing Mrs. Gonzales was a proper threat. Every male under the age of eighty feared her disapproving gaze, which could leave even the most hardened soul squirming like a child.

"I'll be sure to warn him."

3

An animatronic pirate laughed and warned of the curse of Blackbeard's treasure as Gabe parked his car under the sign that read, Pirate Pete's Mini Putt. "Mini golf, really?"

"You asked me to pick someplace fun that I haven't been to in a long time, and I haven't been here in years."

Gabe climbed out of his car, never believing he'd feel dread at the idea of minigolf. "You do know that I am the worst putter in history? Seriously."

"I'm out of practice myself."

When he'd called James to see if he wanted to go out that Saturday, he'd been reading too many articles about blended families and dating in the twenty-first century. He took the advice of some blogger and told James to pick someplace fun that he hadn't been to in a while and keep it a surprise.

"You could be blind with one arm and still putt better than I do."

James laughed. They were heading across the rough gravel of the parking lot when he spotted an old yellow Volvo and an attractive young blond man leaning against it.

"Dylan?"

Dylan looked up from his phone, startled. "Hey! Gabe, Dad? What are you doing here?"

"On a date," James answered. "Thought we'd try something different. What are you doing here?"

"I was waiting on a date."

"Was?"

Dylan held up his phone. "Stood up."

"Temporarily or permanently?" James asked.

"Permanently."

Gabe cringed. "I'm sorry."

Dylan shoved his phone back into his pocket. "It's okay. She was a placeholder really. They're all placeholders until the love of my life comes to her senses and takes me back."

"And how is Catherine these days?" James' tone was completely conversational.

"She's doing really well. Got into the Boston University music program. It's very prestigious and her first choice, so she's excited about that." Dylan actually sounded like someone excited by a friend's success instead of someone whose unrequited love was moving across the country.

"Boston's not exactly close."

"If people can make relationships work long distance, then keeping a temporarily broken-up relationship going should be a piece of cake." Dylan gave a firm little nod in punctuation.

James patted his son on the arm. "I'm sure she'll come around eventually."

"Thanks." Dylan looked between them. "I guess I'll head home, then. You two have fun."

"Wait." Gabe had been considering suggesting a family date at some point in the future, per Tamyra's advice, but this seemed like it might be the perfect opportunity for it. They both turned and looked at him. "Why don't you join us for a round?"

"I don't want to be a third wheel."

James looked between the two of them, then gestured to the course. "Come on. We haven't played a round since you were little. Let me wallow in nostalgia a bit."

Dylan gave a little shake of the head that made him look like James for a moment. "You do that enough already, but okay."

They picked up balls and putters from a bored-looking teenager in a polyester pirate costume. Before Gabe or James could step forward to pay, Dylan pulled out a card covered in punched-out holes.

"I've got a couple of free games."

The teenager took the card and handed Dylan a fresh one, along with their scorecards and little pencils.

"Thanks."

They headed to the practice putting area so a family of six could get a few holes ahead of them. Dylan dropped the red ball he'd picked onto the green and with hardly a pause, knocked the ball into the hole. James took the time to adjust his grip and set his feet but managed to get his in as well. Gabe took a deep breath, adjusted his grip, tried to remember what a dozen pros had attempted to teach him over the years, and proceeded to knock his ball from one side of the green to the other, passing by the cup by at least a foot.

He looked to James. "Told you I was bad at this."

Before James could answer, a phone rang. Gabe reached for his, only to find it quiet.

"Oh!" James fished his phone from his pocket. "Hello?" He took a few steps away from the green while Gabe gave the simple practice putt another try. He only missed the cup by a half foot this time. Dylan was leaning on his club, a smirk on his face.

James finished his call and rejoined them, his brows pulled together. "Um…. Mister McFeely died."

"Who?"

"Our primary mail server crashed. It's called Mister

McFeely. Apparently there was actual smoke coming from the box and no one on campus can get their e-mails. I... um...." James gestured back to the parking lot. "I laid out half the server room as it stands now, and I've got the admin passwords for the backup, and—"

"It's okay. Work happens." Gabe had never been the one to say those words to a date. It felt odd.

"I'm really sorry. This has never.... You know, you two should stay. Not waste the round. I mean, it's your night out."

"It's our night out and—"

Dylan pulled his keys from his pocket and tossed them at James. "Here, take the Lemon Drop. Gabe can give me a lift back. We can bond."

A cold thread of fear slinked up Gabe's spine, but he still smiled. "Sure, no problem."

James nodded, then gave him a kiss on the cheek. "Thank you. I don't know how long—"

"It's fine. Go." James hurried off. "Well, now I know how my dates feel," Gabe mumbled once James was out of earshot. He could not even begin to guess how many dates he'd left due to work (sometimes made-up work), but it had never gone the other way.

"Don't worry about it." Dylan gave him a slap on the back. "It won't happen often. Besides, this way we can chat."

"You want information on the *Budusie tehnologii* deal."

"Can you blame me?"

Gabe tried for one more practice putt and watched it go wide. At least James wouldn't be around to witness his abject humiliation. "And what would you do if you had the information?" Gabe picked up his ball and headed toward the first hole, where a plastic alligator swam around a scummy pond.

"I wouldn't sell it or spread it around. I'm just really curious."

"I'm sure you are. You can keep being curious with everyone else."

Gabe watched as Dylan placed his ball, then hopped it up over a plastic log, landing it inches from the cup.

"How often do you come here?"

"It's the perfect date location."

Gabe tapped his ball, sending it racing across the green and a mile past the cup.

"It's cheap, which is good. It's cute, and girls like cute." Dylan tapped his ball neatly into the cup. "You can talk fairly privately, but you're not sitting in the dark like some pervert. And if you let them win, they'll put out."

That last comment ended what little concentration Gabe had, sending his shot wide and right off the green, where it landed by Dylan's feet.

"Wow, you can't putt, can you?"

"No, no, I can't. Though by your logic, I should be able to get girls that way."

Dylan laughed at him. "Oh no, it works completely the other way." Dylan set the ball back onto the green. "See, if you just play bad, the girl will either think you're lame, and you won't get any, or she'll know you're letting her win, get mad, and you won't get any."

Gabe tried one more putt before giving up and putting a six on the card under his name. They strolled to the next hole.

"What you have to do is let them win by two or three, but you can't just crap out at the end." Dylan placed his ball by a plastic rock and took a swing. The ball raced down the green, bounced off another plastic rock, and went right into the little cup. Gabe sighed. "You have to let them start off ahead, gain on them in the middle, then fall back in the last four holes."

"And to do that, you need to actually be really good."

"Yep." Dylan pulled his ball from the cup while Gabe placed his. "You can do that twice, but then you have to win one, but not by too much so they won't get suspicious, then let them win again. Guaranteed way to get lucky."

Gabe stared at Dylan. It was brilliant in its own oversexed way. "I know men who've had golf listed on their divorce papers, and you've figured out how to use it to get teenaged girls to sleep with you."

Dylan took a grand bow.

"Jesus Christ. No wonder your father is terrified to let you out of the house."

"I'm always careful."

Gabe took his putt and watched it hit a fake rock and roll right back to him. "There are guys at the club who would make you their god."

Gabe took another putt with only marginally better luck.

"Would you like some help?" Dylan offered.

"Every pro the club has ever had has spent hours trying to teach me how to putt. It's a form of hazing for the new guys now."

Dylan grinned. "Yeah, but how many of them use it as a way to get laid?"

"That is a fair point."

"Great. Okay, first off your grip is all wrong." Dylan grabbed Gabe's hands and twisted them around. "It's all about clean lines. Think basic physics. Levers, pendulums. And you're twisting your hands around before you get to the ball. That's why it's going everywhere. Here." Dylan stepped behind him and reached around, gripping Gabe's wrists.

"Dylan. Never tell your father we did this."

"What? Oh." Dylan laughed. "It's okay, you're not my type."

"That doesn't make this look any better."

"Chill. Now spread your legs a little wider, and put your head down."

Gabe locked his jaw, absolutely certain that Dylan knew exactly what he was saying.

"Now, you don't want to change your speed when you swing. Just think of a pendulum, nice and smooth."

Gabe took a swing with Dylan guiding his stroke. The ball still ended up a mile away from the cup, but at least it seemed to go in a slightly straighter line.

"Okay, you are hitting the ball way too hard, but that can be worked on."

Gabe noticed the mother of the family ahead of them on the course giving them a hairy eye. Dylan followed Gabe's look, then draped his arm around Gabe's shoulder and cocked a hip out.

Gabe buried his face in his hand. "Dylan, you are seventeen. Please don't get me arrested. Or in the tabloids."

Dylan laughed again. "Let's just work on your ability to get your ball in the hole."

Gabe ground his teeth. "You are a very dangerous young man."

"I try. Now come on. Let's do it again."

Gabe sighed. He had no reasonable way of getting out of this particular golf lesson, but at least no one from the country club was watching this one and placing bets on how long it'd take his instructor to break. They moved on to the next hole, with Dylan making an easy hole in one. He ran his foot along the Astroturf around the hole. "Okay. See how the turf is worn down here? That means there's less friction on the ball. It'll go faster, so you don't have to hit it as hard. They've recently returfed the back nine, so you'll have to hit it a little harder. Now give it a try."

Gabe spread his legs, adjusted his grip, and barely tapped the ball. It went about a foot. "Okay. That at least was going in the right direction. Just a smidge more force. And remember, pendulums."

Pendulums, Gabe thought. The subtle instruction carried on for a few more holes until Dylan took a step over a piece of plastic driftwood and let out a tiny hiss.

"Are you okay?" he asked quickly, aware of Dylan's bad ankle.

"I'm good." Dylan replied instantly with far too much cheer. Gabe could make out a hair of a limp as they progressed toward the next hole.

"Your ankle. How bad is it? Really?"

Dylan flicked his eyes over for a second before setting his ball in place. "I'm never taking a major league team to a World Series with a bat in my hand." Dylan's voice was flat but sure.

"You're sure of that?"

Dylan bounced his putt around a treasure chest and within six inches of the hole. "Summer after I busted my ankle, Coach Frasier got me a scholarship to a very fancy baseball camp in Arizona. While I was there, he also arranged for a very, very fancy orthopedic surgeon attached to the camp to look at it. Turns out there are a lot of things that show up on an MRI scan and not a basic X-ray."

"How bad?"

"I'll be on a cane by the time I'm thirty and need surgery by thirty-five." Dylan's voice betrayed no emotion. It was just a simple statement of fact, but he didn't look at Gabe as he said it.

"Your father doesn't know, does he? How bad it really is."

"Nope. It would break his heart. And he'd find some way to blame it on himself."

"I'm sorry."

Dylan waved dismissively. "Don't be. I cried my eyes out at fourteen. I'm over it. It'll hold me through college. Possibly even into the minors. If I'm *amazingly, unbelievably* lucky and at no point reinjure myself, and improve my batting average a couple of points, I might even get a season as a small club utility player, but it won't be much beyond that."

"So what's plan B?" Gabe asked, absolutely sure a kid like Dylan would have worked out a plan B by now.

"Plan B is taking a Major League team to the World Series."

Gabe mentally froze for a second as he tried to replay the previous couple of minutes. "I think I missed a bit of conversation."

"Few years back the Cougars lost their shortstop. It's a viciously difficult specialist position, and we were getting hammered without one. I remembered this kid from Little League a year behind me. Brilliant at shortstop. Practically a savant at it. I looked him up, 'randomly' ran into him, we had a little chat, and by the end of the day, I'd talked his parents into applying for a district transfer so he could play shortstop for us."

"What did you offer him? I mean, you couldn't offer him money."

"Nope."

"Playing for a better team?"

"Nope, his team was better in the ranks that season."

"Better scholarship options?"

"Nope."

"Then what?"

"I offered him a chance to play shortstop."

"But he was already playing shortstop?"

"Yes, he was."

"So… you talked him into changing schools so he could do something he was already doing for absolutely nothing extra?" A Cheshire-cat grin slowly spread across Dylan's face. Gabe grinned back. Negotiating something in exchange for something else was a basic human skill. However, talking someone into going out of their way for nothing required a whole different level of talent. "Oh, you are good."

"I'm okay. You'll know when I hit good."

"I bet." If for even one second Gabe had doubted that Dylan

was James' son, that doubt was gone. So many people never got over those childhood disappointments or were unable to cope with sudden turns in their lives. The Maron men, on the other hand, seemed perfectly capable of taking a deep breath and carrying on. "So, business and math classes are really plan A?"

"I'm going to the Show. I'm going to the World Series." Dylan didn't say those words as if they were some vague, wistful hope. It was as sure a plan as getting up in the morning or washing the dishes. "I'm just going to be behind the manager's desk. Maybe not as much fun, but it'll get me there."

"Okay, then."

"I'd offer to score you tickets, but I don't think you'd have a problem getting them on your own."

"No. Probably not."

Gabe noticed a couple on a date quickly working their way up the course behind them. He wondered who was winning. He placed his ball onto the Astroturf and took a swing. The ball rolled down the green, bypassing a plastic skull, slowed, and dropped neatly into the cup.

Gabe's jaw dropped. "Holy crap."

Dylan gave him a pat on the back. "Good." He pointed to the rest of the course. "Now do that nine more times."

To Gabe's surprise, with the exception of a trick shot that involved jumping a small Astroturf hill, he was actually making par on most holes. Almost fifteen years of country club pros sighing over his putting, and from ninety minutes on a minigolf course, he'd figured out how not to twist his wrists, shepherd the ball, overcorrect, or knock it right off the green. His level of personal shock was profound.

Dylan made the final shot into a treasure chest, then started adding up the scores.

"How'd I do?"

"Well, if you were a girl, you probably wouldn't be returning my phone calls."

"Let me see." Dylan handed over the card. "You know, I've done worse. I've done lots worse."

"I'm sorry."

"It's okay. Hell, if you were older, I'd offer to buy you a drink for the lessons."

"I think my father might object."

"Yeah. How about dinner? We can get your father some takeout as well if it looks like he's going to be late." Gabe's phone beeped. "Speaking of." He looked at the text. "Yes, the mail server actually did start smoking, but someone shoved a plastic bag over the smoke detector before the fire suppressors went off, which would have destroyed the entire server room. He's not going to be home for a while."

"Takeout it is."

———

A LATE FOG had rolled in, giving a shimmer to the lights dotted around the campus and deepening the shadows of the columns decorating the grander buildings. Gabe followed the little map Dylan had drawn for him. The occasional student scurried by, either laden down with books or weaving badly. He expected the small gray building that housed the support department to be locked, but the door opened and the elevator took him down a story. From there it was a matter of following his nose. Even with the smell of Thai chilies coming from the bag he held, he could make out the odor of fried electronics. It was a smell that had permeated his dorm room for one memorable six-month stretch. He found a door labeled "Server Room" propped open with a battered copy of *DOS for Dummies* and followed his nose through.

Inside, LED lights blinked from row after row of server racks. Lengths of wires were draped across the floor in ways that certainly violated OSHA regulations. A few missing floor panels revealed even more wiring, and there was an incessant hum created by hundreds of cooling fans and industrial air-conditioning. There were two pieces of paper taped to the first rack. The first was a large black-and-white photocopied picture of James glaring daggers at whoever was taking the picture. The other one read:

DO NOT
TOUCH ANYTHING!
Yes, this means you.
No, you don't know
what you're doing.
You think you do, but you don't.
NO TOUCHING!!
(and no food or drink)

GABE HEARD some voices and made his way down the rows until he found James and a few other staffers kneeling beside a large server box with a very old TechPrim logo on the side. He recognized most of them from attending Dave's (James' least effective team member) Indian shotgun wedding. The box was cracked open, and on the floor next to it was what might have been a circuit board in a past life. Now the plastic was blackened and bubbled in places. There was also a power supply and some other bits and pieces that Gabe couldn't name, though after all these years he should be able to.

"You know, I could make some calls and try to get someone down here?"

James and his staff snapped their heads up from their work. "No!" they answered, pretty much in unison. "Don't you dare," James continued. "We have needed a new server here for years now, but as long as we were keeping this one limping along, they weren't going to get us a new one."

"Got it."

"The magic smoke has now very literally escaped." James' team nodded in agreement. "We just need to get the backups stable."

"But not too stable," Zippy said quickly, and there were more nods of agreement.

"Understood." Gabe looked down at the bag in his hand. "I dropped Dylan off but figured you'd be late, so I brought dinner here."

Chris made an "awww" noise as James got up, brushing off his dusty hands on his pants.

He took the bag, their fingers touching for a second.

"Hey there," a voice called down the rows. Gabe turned around as Dave approached, carrying a black plastic bag.

"Dave."

Dave gave him a nod. "Here we go." He handed the bag to James, who opened it up and pulled out a few plastic cups and a bottle of bright pink, cheap-looking strawberry daiquiri mix, blatantly disregarding on-campus alcohol rules as well as server-room food and beverage consumption policies.

James passed around the cups, including one for Gabe. "Now, no one in this room ever speaks of this. It did not happen. No tweeting it, no Facebooking it, no writing it in your little pink diary. Nothing. Got it?"

There were nods as James twisted open the bottle. A cloying sweet smell was undercut by harsh alcohol mixed with the smell of chilies and burned electronics. James poured some into every cup, then raised his.

"To Mister McFeely, an old war horse of a mail server. He served us well through thick and thin. He processed a million offers of cheap Viagra; Reply to Alls that should have been Reply to None; he fought off viruses that crippled lesser machines. But for everything there is a season, and his winter has come and passed, and it is now time to salvage as much of his memory as we can and commit the rest of him to the sands of time."

Everyone raised their cups and drank to the pile of metal and plastic that had received a more poetic sendoff then any server could possibly hope for.

The daiquiri mix tasted surprisingly like strawberry cough syrup, and Gabe fought not to make a face. Everyone else tipped it back. Gabe was no longer willing to believe he was ever that young.

"Okay." James rubbed his eyes and collected the cups. "Let's violate the last of the expired warranty on this thing, then start pulling up cables."

"I'll head out and leave you to it."

"Thanks for dinner. I guess we'll rain check the rest?"

"It's not a problem. Are you sure there's nothing I can do about… that?" Gabe waved his hand over the mess.

"I suppose if TechPrim sales wants to coincidentally stop by on Monday morning sporting a good deal on a new server or two with a reasonable extended warranty and support plan, I'm pretty sure they'd make a sale."

Gabe smiled. "I'll send a memo." Nearly everyone else had their noses up to a monitor or in a piece of hardware. He leaned in and gave James a quick peck and a squeeze of the hand before heading out, the taste of alcohol and artificial strawberry flavor still thick in his mouth.

GABE WAS NEVER 100 percent certain why he hung around the country club. No one really liked him all that much, and he didn't particularly like anyone there. At the start it was a place to network and make connections, at least that was what he'd been told, but now he had more of those than he should ever need. He guessed that in the end, it provided a decent hiding place. He could have a cup of coffee, sit in the sun, and listen to birds chirp even while drafting out proposals and goal strategies on a Saturday morning.

A shadow suddenly fell across his notebook and into his light. He looked up at Simon Fredell's artificially white teeth that were a natural match for his artificially thick hair. Gabe felt low-grade irritation and revulsion at Simon's existence roll around his stomach. The man was the biggest tool that Gabe had to associate with and was sitting, unknowingly, on the two most important technology patents of the last twenty years.

"Gabe, how are you?" Simon's grin crawled its way across his face, unnaturally wide.

There was not a single drop of honesty in that smile that Gabe could detect. "I'm fine, thanks for asking."

"Hey, I don't suppose you'd be up for a round on the course?"

"Are you serious?" Simon had never asked him to golf. On the few occasions they had golfed together, it had always been someone else extending the invitation.

"Burt dropped out. We need another person for the foursome."

"And your portfolio is doing so badly this month that the only way you can make yourself feel better is by kicking my ass around the golf course?"

Simon laughed a laugh as fake as the rest of him. "Come on, Juarez, put the work aside for a couple of hours before you give yourself a stroke."

Gabe stared at Simon and briefly pictured throttling him with a mouse cable, but as Tamyra liked to remind him, he still needed to occasionally play nice with the other kids.

He smiled. "Sure."

"Great. We tee off in an hour."

A HINT of a breeze rustled the leaves of the oaks lining the fairway. Gabe adjusted his grip and aimed for the little red flag marking the green. This was the easy bit. He'd been called a driving savant. He could hit the green in a gale without a second thought. At least on the shorter courses. He swung and watched the ball arch into the air, fade slightly in the breeze, and come down neatly on the green.

Simon looked through his binoculars. "Jesus, Gabe, if you could putt half as well as you drive you could have gone pro." Simon had landed in the rough while Luke and Mark had both made it to the edge of the green.

As they strolled along to the green, Gabe listened to the three other men chat away about business, their wives, portfolios. Luke had bought a new boat to retire on. Mark was thinking about another divorce. The gossip was pretty much the only reason Gabe even tried to golf. It was a stupid game, whacking a little lumpy ball around a big park with a bendy stick.

Luke tapped his ball neatly in once they got to the green. Mark got close but would need another putt, and Simon managed to whack his out of the rough and onto the green. Gabe pulled out his putter.

"We might as well put our feet up, guys," Simon said, and the other two laughed.

Gabe walked up to his ball that sat only a couple feet from the hole. He went to take his putt, then stopped. He took a deep breath. He pictured Astroturf and a plastic pirate staring at him. He reset his grip, squared his shoulders, and squared his legs.

Smooth, he thought. *Not too strong. Simple machines.*

He swung, there was a quiet tap, and the ball rolled forward at a nice even speed and plunked into the cup.

He looked over at the guys. There were three open jaws. "If you all keep standing there with your mouths hanging open, I'm going to start getting ideas."

Three sets of teeth clacked shut. "That was a fluke," Simon stated.

Gabe gave a casual shrug. Internally he was doing one hell of a victory dance.

Simon and Mark both putted out, and the four of them moved on. Once again Gabe had no trouble hitting the green, but the ball bounced to the far edge. "Okay, Gabe, let's see if you can do that again."

Gabe looked at the space between his ball and the cup. "Nope. Too far." Gabe took his swing. *Not too hard*, he reminded himself. *Just get close, don't overshoot.*

Gabe made it within a foot. On his next turn, he dropped it in neatly. Simon stared at him. "Are you working with a new coach or something?"

Gabe tried to look innocent. "Just feeling lucky today."

"Luck? You have never once shot better than, what was it, fifteen over par? And that was years ago."

Gabe looked at the putter in his hand and for a half second visualized cracking Simon's skull open with it. "You know what, I am feeling so lucky, I bet you I can par in. Or even under." Mark and Luke both laughed, but Simon stared at him quietly. Simon still owed him almost forty grand from a poorly-thought-out bet the year before. If he thought he could win that money back, it gave Gabe some leverage. Gabe knew he was taking a big chance on his new skills, but it was the best opportunity he'd gotten to get his hands on Simon's company, Solar Flare, and he did not want to let it slip by.

"A bet. Okay. And what do you want if hell freezes over and you golf under par?"

Gabe tilted his head back, appearing to think for a moment,

then smirked. "I shoot under par and you sell me Solar Flare Technologies."

"What the hell would you want that for?"

"I've seen the way you treat your employees. I'm looking at it like a puppy rescue."

Simon looked like he wanted to laugh. "You're such a fucking Commie, Juarez."

"Yeah." Gabe slid his putter back into his bag. "But I'm a fucking rich Commie."

"Okay, and when I win this bet, what do I get?"

Gabe pretended to think again. "I'll forget about that forty you owe me from last year." Simon looked at him hard. "Works out for you either way."

"Okay, then, it's a deal. Witnesses?" Luke and Mark both nodded. "Then let's play."

They moved on to the next tee. While Gabe waited for his turn to drive, he tried to visualize every good shot he'd had the other day. He tried to remember exactly how he had been standing, how the putter felt in his hands, where the ball and club head touched.

He drove without thinking, still working on the visualizations. The four of them began to walk.

"Hey, Gabe." Gabe pulled himself out of his own head and paid attention to Luke. "What's with the whole coming out now? I mean we're not that uptight around here, don't think anyone would have cared."

Gabe stopped dead in his tracks. The three turned to look at him. "I came out when I was sixteen. Sixteen!" He didn't really care if his voice went up several octaves. "My mother found my *Playgirls*, threw a fit, and sent me to a priest. I haven't been 'in' in decades, certainly not for a single second I've known the lot of you."

"Really?" All three looked confused.

"You've met some of my boyfriends. André?"

"Wasn't he your PA?" Luke asked.

"Ming?"

Mark suddenly looked confused. "Ming was a he?"

"I lived with Gregory Smith, for fuck's sake!" Gabe was very close to flat-out yelling.

"He was gay?"

Gabe slapped his hand to his face. "Wow. My sociology professor was right. You lot really can't see past your preconceived heteronormative world views, can you?" They looked at him blankly. "Guys, in 2006, 15.4 percent of San Francisco residents considered themselves gay, lesbian, or bisexual, and guess what, some of them are capable of driving out of the city limits, over one of many bridges, and swinging a country club membership. Think about it." Gabe grabbed his bag and marched toward the next hole with purpose.

For the next four holes, Gabe ignored the other three men and turned all his focus to his game. Before every putt he ran a hand over the grass to work out the speed. He carefully gauged the strength needed for each and worked on his form, the whole time picturing treasure chests and laughing plastic pirates. By the seventh hole, he was one over par.

"Are you sure you're not hustling us, Juarez?" Simon asked.

"Yes, Simon. I've pretended to play like crap for over a decade so I can win a bankrupt second-rate tech company off you."

The look Simon gave him was what his grandmother would call "the evil eye." "I wouldn't put it past you."

Gabe grinned. "I've been working with a new trainer."

Mark made a chip shot out of the sand trap. Mark was the opposite of Gabe. He could putt like a dream, but his balls were always magically attracted to sand and water. "Did you really live with Gregory Smith?" Simon asked suddenly.

"Yes, I really did."

"I remember him being a complete asshole."

Gabe resisted making a comment about pots and kettles. "He was a giant asshole. He was also handsome and very charming and could be quite persuasive when he wanted something."

Luke made his putt from a good fifteen feet away. "He always used to brag that he was going to scoop up this funny little tech company he'd found called TechPrim and make a fortune selling off the patents. We all just thought it was a kinda stupid name."

Gabe grit his teeth. He was never going to live that down. "It was a typo, okay? It was three in the morning, and I was tired when I submitted the trademark registration. And yes, he was trying to get TechPrim, by any means necessary."

Mark finally made his putt.

"Was the sex at least worth it?" It would be Simon who would ask that.

"No. No, it wasn't."

After the tenth hole, Gabe felt the conversation flowing back his way. He'd managed to make a birdie putt and was now at par.

"Juarez, not that you're going to win this, but if you did get Solar Flare, what the hell would you do with it?"

"Gut it," Gabe lied smoothly. "A couple of your engineers would be good additions to our battery enhancement team. Buying the whole company is a fuckload easier than trying to work around the restraint of trade clauses in their contracts. And TechPrim still has enough R&D going that we can find a spot for the rest of them."

Gabe hit his drive. He watched it sail into the air, land on the green, bounce twice, and roll neatly into the hole. He threw his arms into the air.

"You've got to be shitting me," Simon whined.

"Like I said, new trainer." Shots like that were pure luck, and everyone knew it, but Gabe gladly took that luck. It made him two strokes under, a buffer, which he was happy to have with seven holes to go.

By the next hole, Gabe was thankful for that buffer as he overshot his first putt and found the sand trap, then skinned the ball out of the sand trap into the rough. Coming out of the rough put him on the far edge of the green, putting him over par by the end. He heard Simon snicker.

Gabe took a deep breath, then indulged a quick moment to visualize drowning Simon in a water hazard, then set about trying to visualize the rest of the game.

Within another two holes, Gabe was nearly back at par. Mark and Luke had stopped talking. Even Simon had given up on his version of wit. It was now really about one thing: pride.

I am a heterosexual teenaged boy, Gabe thought. *If I make this putt, an attractive girl will sleep with me.*

He let out his breath slowly, then tapped the ball. It rolled across the expanse of green, rimmed the cup, and popped back out. He decided one of the few positives to come out of years of playing badly was that when shit like that happened you had less of an urge to break a titanium club over your knee.

Simon didn't fare much better. Not that Simon's final score had anything to do with the bet, but as Gabe improved, Simon seemed to feel the need to do that much better. Luke and Mark didn't even seem to be trying anymore.

Gabe teed off on the last hole and watched his ball arc once more into the air. It hit the green, bounced, and rolled to the far edge.

"Shit," Gabe breathed.

Simon gave him a less-than-sympathetic pat on the back. "Don't worry about it, Juarez. It's still your best round ever."

"It's not over yet." It was true that Gabe only had two strokes left to keep under par, but he was sure he could manage that.

They got to the green. Gabe sighted down the ball to the

cup. It was at least fifteen feet. He ran his fingers along the grass. It was still slightly damp from the morning fog. He spread his legs and set his body. *Simple machines.*

He had two. He just needed to get as close as possible. He pulled back his arms and tapped the ball. The ball rolled. It slowed. It perched on the edge of the cup. Gabe held his breath, and there was a plink as it dropped into the cup.

"You are fucking shitting me." That smug little smile was nowhere to be seen on Simon's now slack face.

Gabe twirled his putter around, then slid it back in his bag, looking as cool as anything. In his head he was doing a dance of joy, possibly to "U Can't Touch This" that would have gotten him thrown out just for looking like a total moron.

"I'll get the papers sent around Monday morning. Don't worry, you'll get a good price." He wasn't even trying to keep the grin off his face as Simon turned interesting shades of red.

"Fuck it! Okay, who is this trainer, and how much does he charge, because if he can teach *you* to play like *that*, then he should be able to make me a pro."

"Sorry, he's very exclusive, invite only. But tell you what, boys, I'll buy lunch."

THE LAUNDROMAT TELEVISION was on mute, but someone had found the remote and put on the subtitles. James didn't read Spanish as well as he spoke it. Fortunately the plot wasn't exactly hard to follow. Ernesto's father was threatening to cut him out of the will unless he agreed in writing never to give any money to Gabriella, whose mother had been nothing but a gold digger, at least according to Ernesto's father.

James reached into his pocket and counted the change with his fingers. There were some towels in the load, which always needed extra time in the dryer. He supposed he could get out the worst of the damp and dry them the rest of the way in the kitchen.

His phone vibrated in his pocket against the change.

Can I come over? At the Club. About a half hour away.

James checked the countdown on the dryer, then which part of the wash cycle his last load of laundry was in. If he folded the laundry at home, he could make it back up in half an hour. He'd have to iron some of his work shirts.

He wondered who did Gabe's ironing. He'd never seen any kind of housekeeper while at Gabe's place, but he wasn't actually there all that often. He still doubted Gabe had the time to fold his own shirts that always looked perfectly pressed. Or mop his own floors or clean his own windows.

James secretly hated folding laundry. Something about it grated him to the very bone. Someone to fold it for him would be nice. But that was never going to happen. He glanced back up at the TV. Gabriella dramatically wiped the sweat away as she bent over a hot stove in a small kitchen. Her hair still looked perfect, and her blouse clung to her body in a way that just hinted at what was underneath.

James ran his fingers through his own hair. The heat from the washers and dryers always made it stand up at strange angles. He looked down at his phone. Dylan was going out. James couldn't think of any good reason for Gabe not to come over.

Sure.

GABE KNOCKED on the door to James' apartment in a jaunty rhythm. He'd been bouncing all day; for a while he'd felt as if he could have run all the way to James' building. The joy of banishing that smug look from Simon's face was only seconded by the knowledge that Solar Flare was going to change the world and make him an unbelievable fortune in the process.

Dylan opened the door. "Hey, is your dad here?"

"He's finishing up the laundry. He should be up in a minute." Dylan stepped aside, letting him in.

"Great. Actually—" He pulled Dylan into a back-slapping hug, nearly taking him off the floor.

"Okay." Dylan blinked at him. "What was that for?"

"I shot one under par."

"Okay. Good."

"Oh no, you don't understand, previously my best game was twelve *over*. In fact, this is for you." Gabe pulled out a few hundred from his wallet and held it out to Dylan. "Years of high-paid pros completely failed to teach me what you managed to get across in ninety minutes on a minigolf course. That is how much those pros make for ninety minutes of instruction." In truth it was close to double, but Dylan deserved a hell of a tip.

Dylan counted the money. "And I've been busting my ass playing baseball all this time? I picked the wrong sport."

"And not only did I shoot under par, but I won a bet I made with this *total* asshole named Simon. Absolute tool who has done nothing but try to give me shit for damn near a decade. I hate him, and I will take the look on his loser face to my grave."

Dylan had a grin of his own. "I'm glad I could help."

Gabe heard keys rattle in the door, but before he could get to it, James let himself in, hefting a basket of laundry. Gabe took it from his hands, set it aside, closed the door, and pressed James against it, locking their lips together. After a few seconds, Dylan loudly cleared his throat. Gabe took a half step back but didn't turn around. "Hi. I'm having a really good Saturday. Let me take you out someplace nice in the city. How about Ame? I can absolutely get us last-second reservations."

"Hi. Okay." James looked startled, but Gabe didn't care.

Frankly, if they didn't have a very inappropriate audience, he'd have ripped off James' clothes right then and there.

"Great. Go get changed. Actually, I'll help."

Dylan put his fingers in his ears and started singing "Yellow Submarine" loudly and completely out of tune.

Gabe ignored it and dragged James down to the bedroom.

"Why the good mood?"

Gabe threw open James' wardrobe and quashed the urge to take him clothes shopping instead of to dinner. "I played a round of golf today and scored under par."

"This is about golf?"

"No." Gabe pulled out the silky green shirt James had worn their first time together. "This is about golfing under par, something I have never once done by the way, and in doing so winning a bet with Simon."

"The tool?"

"Yes, the tool. And by winning the bet, he has agreed to sell me a crappy little tax shelter tech company he owns." He pulled out James' best-looking trousers.

"Would this be the company with the patents you really wanted? The big game changer."

He picked James up, spun him around, and kissed him hard. "I've got the patents," he whispered. "Take a good look at the world, because it is five years and one Russian trade deal away from a revolution that will change it forever and for the better."

"And make you rich?"

"I'm already rich. This…." He kissed James again. "You know what, I'll tell you about it later. I promise you it's a good thing." He pulled off James' work shirt and flung it across the room. "Now get changed before I just take you on that tiny little bed of yours and scandalize the whole damn building."

JAMES HAD ONLY QUICKLY SCANNED the menu of Ame and was now fiddling with the edge of his napkin. Gabe could already guess that James would order the cheapest thing from the appetizer menu and claim he wasn't all that hungry. Gabe had had other boyfriends who pulled that, but they'd all been verging on eating disorders.

"Are you okay?" James had seemed distracted since they got to the restaurant.

"What? Oh, I'm fine." James flashed a quick smile, but Gabe didn't buy it.

"How's Dylan doing?" That often seemed the top of the list of James' worries, even when he had nothing to worry about.

"He's fine."

"Good." Gabe reached into his pocket and pulled out a slim little black case that fit neatly in his hand. "I've got something for you." James put down his napkin and opened the case. He blinked a few times. Gabe grinned. "It's our new P22X phone."

James took it out. It wasn't much thicker than an old 3 1/2-inch floppy disc. The screen had a patented coating that would not pick up fingerprints, and the case was a shade of black reminiscent of the obelisk in *2001: A Space Odyssey*, with the TechPrim logo subtly embossed on the back. It had more computing power than most of last season's laptops. It had more memory, more battery power, and a higher grade of HD camera than the standard P22. TechPrim had "leaked" a half dozen fake P22s to throw off their competitors, to catch them flat-footed when the official model hit the shelves. When the P22 had hit the shelves the previous month, Gabe had stood on his balcony and listened to the sounds of the competition screaming in frustration way off across the valley. TechPrim had already grabbed a serious chunk of the high-end smart phone market and would be dominant by the end of the year.

"And it has been thoroughly tested, and it should never drop calls and should actually ring when someone calls you."

James turned it around in his hand. "I've seen the ads for this."

"Yeah, marketing's been patting themselves on the back pretty hard." Marketing had been insufferable. "Turn it on." Gabe had programed in his number, Dylan's, and a few others he thought James might need.

James looked at him. "I've looked at these. This is several months' rent."

"You need a new phone."

James put the phone carefully back in its case and closed his eyes. "I don't think this is going to work. I'm sorry."

"What?"

James stood while Gabe tried to process what had just happened. He'd had a lot of practice at rapidly backtracking relationships to see where he fucked up, but he was missing something big here. He stood and chased after James, who had already made it to the bus stop halfway down the block.

"James…. Wait, what are you doing?"

"I'm waiting for a bus," James replied quite calmly, not looking at Gabe. "That's what people like me do, we catch buses and trains."

"Please, what did I do? If you don't like the phone—"

James took a deep breath. "I don't need a sugar daddy."

"What?" Gabe could have sworn a brick slammed into his chest at James' words, completely derailing what few thoughts he had.

"I am thankful for the way you helped Dylan the other day, but I don't need… things from you. I don't need to be saved. I am quite capable of living within my means and taking care of myself and Dylan, and have been doing so for a long time."

"It's just a phone."

James finally turned to him. "And what happens when my car breaks? Will you get me a new one?"

"I'd love to! Your car terrifies me."

"That is not the point." James' words were clear and crisp. A bus pulled up, and the door opened. Gabe threw himself between it and James.

"Wait, James. Wait. Can we talk, please?"

"Are you getting on?" the driver yelled out.

"He'll catch another one," Gabe snapped over his shoulder. James folded his arms, giving Gabe a very annoyed and paternal look that was causing his spine to quickly shrivel. "I understand what you're saying. Please… just." It had been a long time since Gabe had made the effort to try to talk someone out of leaving him. He needed to stall for time. "Dinner? I promised you dinner." James' look didn't falter. "At least let me drive you home. The buses on the weekends are full of weirdos."

For the first time in his life, Gabe prayed for red lights as he made his way slowly through San Francisco traffic and toward the bridge. James sat silent next to him, staring out the window. It wasn't the "I hate you, and I'm giving you the silent treatment" silence he'd gotten from past boyfriends. This silence seemed almost sad.

Sugar daddy. Those were the words James had used. Those words twisted around inside him, turning his stomach, and driving out nearly every other thought. He wanted to argue it, but on some sick level, it fit. He'd just wanted to get James a new phone. It had been as self-serving as anything else. And wouldn't he have looked like a cheap bastard if he'd gotten one of their stock standard phones? He was the CFO. What was the point of a chronically busy lifestyle if you couldn't get your hands on the newest toys first and give them to your boyfriend? Your boyfriend who had flat-out said he didn't want things.

But there's a difference between wanting to get things for yourself and accepting gifts. Right?

Sugar daddy. Gabe's grip on the wheel tightened, and he slowed to five below the speed limit. He couldn't think of what to say. Every idea that popped into his head sounded patronizing, needy, mean, or weird.

The lights on the freeway went by too fast as they neared James' exit. He needed more time. He pulled up in front of James' building. James didn't jump out right away, and Gabe took it as the first good sign of the trip.

"Can I call you later?" Gabe kept his voice low.

"Gabe, I—"

"Please? Just a call? That's it. I promise."

James took a deep shuddering breath, gave a tight nod, then jumped from the car, all but running to the security gate, not once looking back.

DYLAN WAS out for the night, and the only light in the apartment came from the streetlamps outside. James didn't bother turning on the lights as he made his way across the living room and down the hall. He was glad Dylan was out. He'd be able to tell something was wrong; he'd want all the details on what happened. He'd want a conversation, and James really wasn't interested in what Dylan would have to say on the matter.

Actually, he knew exactly what Dylan would say. *"Why didn't you take the phone?"*

Dylan didn't understand. He'd been too young to notice judgmental looks and whispers, or the scraping for pennies at the grocery store. *"Why didn't you take the phone?"*

First it would be the phone, but Gabe was rich. He wouldn't understand. There was nothing stopping him from getting them a new computer, new clothes, a car. It would be too easy to get used to it. Too easy to get reliant on it. He hadn't made it this far only to put his and Dylan's upkeep into someone else's hands. Hands that could vanish as quickly as they arrived.

Why had he even told Gabe he could call? It was just leaving the door open. Leaving himself open.

James walked into the bathroom, shoved a washcloth in his mouth, screamed, then went to bed.

4

Fabric rustled softly against fabric and wooden hangers occasionally clacked against each other as Gabe went through his closet. He was supposed to be picking a suit for some formal evening function. He couldn't even remember what it was despite having been told just hours earlier. And in all honesty, he didn't care.

He hadn't called James. It had been a full day, and he still didn't have a clue as to what to say to get James back. He had driven home as slowly as possible the night before, hoping James would call, invite him back, and he wouldn't be too far away when it happened.

When previous boyfriends had walked out, and there had been plenty, he let them walk out, and if he could be bothered, he bought forgiveness with something nice. Like a new phone. Not that he was trying to buy James off. He just wanted him to have a phone that would pick up calls when the humidity went above 50 percent. And James had gotten angry.

His own emotions had been swinging between confused, depressed, and briefly angry. He'd thrown up when a dark little voice deep in his mind, that sounded like a nightmare, had whispered, "He should be grateful."

His hand landed on the shoulder of a blue suit jacket that had been shoved to the far end of the closet. He took it out. Double-breasted, blue but a half shade too bright, and more than a decade out of fashion, especially in Silicon Valley.

He had complained the whole time he'd been fitted for it. He'd felt like a pincushion or a chalkboard. His eyes had watered at the price of a necktie in that little shop that was down some San Francisco back alley. Gregory had promised him he'd look great. Gregory had made him a lot of promises.

Gabe ran his fingers down the lapels, a little too wide, really. Gregory had been the one who looked better in wide lapels. A European cut, making his shoulders look a little too broad. It was good fabric. Wool. The thread count could have been higher. Not that Gabe had known that at the time. He'd glimpsed the bill a second before it went into Gregory's wallet. It shocked him that someone would pay that much for a suit just for him.

He glanced back into his closet. The suit that had hung next to the blue one was a dark charcoal wool with a subtle herringbone weave. He'd bought it the previous November in London for a couple thousand pounds. He'd been introduced to the tailor by one of the members of the House of Lords, whom he had met while negotiating TechPrim's first major international deal. That had been six months after Gregory left town. Six months of Gabe flying the company solo once again.

Gabe stepped from his bedroom onto the balcony surrounding his penthouse condo, holding his slightly too-bright blue suit. The wind was cool, but it tasted clean. He took the jacket off the hanger and chucked five hundred dollars of tailoring down to the sidewalk below. Someone would pick it up. Maybe it would be a good color on them.

He went back inside, grabbed his phone, and dialed James'

number. It rang seven times, and Gabe was about to hang up, not wanting to leave a message.

"Hello?" James' voice was tentative, and Gabe was so happy to hear it.

"Hi. It's me. Look can we talk for a second? That's all, talk."

TAMYRA DROPPED several binders in front of Gabe with a heavy thud. He winced and listened carefully for any crack or creaking of the wood. He did love his desk, with its mother-of-pearl inlay and climbing vines carved into the legs. It stood as a daily reminder of his first major victory in the business world.

"These came up from the fifth floor. Why do you want to buy Solar Flare, other than the fact that it pisses off someone you hate?" She'd been cranky at him since Monday when he refused to discuss his own crankiness, even if her guess that he and James had fought was spot-on. Gabe was admittedly less cranky since he'd talked James into seeing him again, but that was still several days away. Plenty of time for James to change his mind.

He flipped open the top binder. It was a rundown of everything Solar Flare owned and held, from employee contracts to the pens in their stationery cupboards. He'd half forgotten the whole reason he'd gone out on that disastrous dinner. Luckily he'd sent a memo down to fifth before heading to see James.

He had to give his teams credit. They could do their due diligence and still cut a check in record time. At this point they were probably grateful to buy up a company where everything was in English, and one that had been sold so often half the work was already done. He dug through the binders until he found the patents. Without saying a word, he pulled two from the stack and handed them to Tamyra.

She read them over, then read them again. "Will this actually work?"

"I showed it to R&D. They nearly wet themselves. You get more power out of a square foot of those solar cells than an entire bank of the ones currently on the market. And that other thingy will charge batteries, even at the low voltage you get from solar, with only a tiny fraction of lost power. We figure out how to miniaturize it, and we can have our phones charged in five minutes."

She gave the patents one more read over before smiling at him. "You are a complete bastard. This has been your game plan the whole time."

Gabe grinned. It was a rare thing to ever get a step ahead of Tamyra. "No. This is just the really awesome chocolate buttercream frosting all over the cake."

"Have you eaten lunch yet?"

"No. But now I really want cake."

Tamyra slid the sheets back into the binder. "Why don't you grab a couple boxes of donuts, take a ten-minute drive, and tell the good people of Solar Flare they have a loving new owner? You can personally explain their new contracts."

"I do get a lot of hugs when I do that." And Gabe felt like he could use some hugs, lots of hugs, even ones from strangers. It was one of the few real feel-good things he got to do. When he handed someone a contract that let them make their mortgage payments, they got very happy. Throw vision and dental coverage on top of that, and he had ended up in the middle of some very weepy spontaneous group hugs over the last few years. And as a group, engineers didn't cry pretty. There was usually snot involved.

"And then you can come back here and work on your Russian."

That killed the hint of a good mood he'd worked up. "Why am I doing that to myself?"

"I have absolutely no fucking idea."

———

GABE MADE his way carefully up San Pablo Avenue, navigating the thick Thursday evening traffic. People were trying to bypass the rush-hour jams on the freeway, clogging the surface streets as they did, but Gabe was in no great rush. It had taken considerable time, effort, and every drop of his negotiation skills to talk James into a second try at dinner. He was determined not to screw this one up.

As they left Berkeley, the canopy of large trees shading the organic cafés and coffee shops vanished. It became rows of little ethnic restaurants, muffler repair shops, minimalls, and second-string fast-food joints, all looking dusty and worn.

Gabe made a point to double check that the restaurant he wanted to take James to was still in business. He hadn't been in several years despite it once being a favorite. It was one of those tiny places with excellent food that always seemed on the verge of going under. He'd even called ahead for a reservation despite never having seen it filled on a weekday.

As they neared the Potrero Avenue intersection, Gabe pulled over right in front of a neon sign advertising Thai cuisine.

"Here?" James asked, looking at the small weathered brick building attached to a boarded-up pawn shop.

"Here."

The little bells that dangled in front of the door chimed. Gabe looked around, glad that nothing had changed. There were plastic flowers on the tables, and Thai soap operas showing on a mute TV. It was light-years from the Michelin-starred minimalistic elegance of their last failed meal. He felt himself relax as the smells from the kitchen and some nice memories rolled over him.

They were immediately approached by the smiling elderly lady who ran the place while her husband did the cooking. He never managed to learn her name, even when he was a semiregular customer. She sat them by the window and quickly took their drink orders.

Gabe looked over the menu as the BART train rumbled by nearly overhead, completely drowning out the sound of the restaurant music and the traffic outside.

James had yet to make any proper eye contact and looked intently over the dinner menu. The dishes on offer probably hadn't changed since the mid '90s. "What's good here?" he asked, still not looking up.

"Anything. The *larb gai* is the best in the Bay." It was, but he also knew James nearly always went for the chicken salad. Cheapest thing on most menus.

"Okay."

Gabe waved to the waitress, who took their order with a smile. James ordered the *larb gai*, while Gabe got the *nam sod*.

James looked around at the little tables and Thailand tourism posters on the wall. "How'd you find this place?"

It was an obvious attempt at polite conversation on James' part, but it was a good enough place for Gabe to start. He hadn't planned out exactly what he was going to say but knew what he wanted to get across.

"I grew up about fifteen minutes from here." James turned his head slightly toward the hills with their big suburban houses and million-dollar views of the city. "Other way." James gave him a questioning look. Gabe took a deep breath. "I grew up in Richmond, on the wrong side of 23rd. Hell, we were on the wrong side of 9th, right down near the refinery. There were ten bullet holes in our garage door, and if you put your thumb over the top one, the rest looked kinda like Virgo. I've got two cousins in Quentin, one for assault with possession and the other for assault with intent, and both of those were plea-bargains. Only one of my sisters was over eighteen when she had her first kid. And... I forget all that. I try my damnedest to forget all of that. I surround myself with people who help me forget that. I have a bottle of prescription migraine medication that I only take when talking to my cousins' lawyers. I try to convince myself that I was born fully formed just the way I am. And I am sorry. I didn't think. I forgot. When I was eighteen, I turned down a scholarship for low-income Latino kids because the academic requirements were only 3.5, and I had a 4.2. It felt too much like charity, and I'd fought too damn hard to get where I was on my own. If someone had tried to hand me something like that phone, I would have walked away too."

Gabe closed his eyes and lowered his head, even as the words came out of his mouth.

"Actually no, that's a lie. There was someone who I let give me things and take me places, make me promises, and I should have turned and run as fast and as far as I could. He spun me around so hard I didn't know who I was or which way was up anymore or who I was even supposed to be. And when I finally got out of that, I swore I would never become like him, but here I am now, dancing on the edge of it. I honestly didn't think about... I just made a note to myself that you needed a new phone, and I didn't even think about how you might feel about it or if you even wanted one. It was selfish and presumptuous on my part, and I am really sorry."

James traced his finger around one of the tropical flowers printed on the plastic tablecloth, staying silent for nearly a minute, his eyes fixed to the table. "I've... I've had to justify to someone, often myself, every decision I have ever made since I was fourteen, because if I don't, someone with the ability to make that decision will take it away from me. Defensive is sort of a default setting." James took a deep breath and finally looked up. "And I do need a new phone."

Gabe reached over and gently placed his hand over James', trying not to show the absolute shattering relief that slammed into his system. He wasn't on stable ground yet, though. "Your phone is an 8A-37X Phantom. That phone was recalled, in total, within three weeks of hitting the market. It was the biggest fuckup in TechPrim history. If we were on a stock market, our share price would have tanked. People got fired, departments got restructured, entire chapters of our best practices guide were rewritten, we broke off contracts with major partners, and we gave a full refund or new phone to everyone who bought one. I checked the records, and only a couple of hundred, globally, didn't get returned. Legally TechPrim owes you a refund or a new phone. I don't even know how you got that one."

"It was secondhand."

Gabe gave James' hand a small squeeze. "Please. Whatever is between you and me is between you and me, but on a company pride and legality level, I can't let you keep that phone. Please? And I promise, if we keep going, I will consult you before ever trying to give you anything else. I swear."

James stared at him, his face unreadable, while Gabe pleaded with his eyes as much as possible. "Okay. But that's it. Don't try to get me a new car or something."

Gabe cringed a little. "Your birthday?" He tried to make it sound like a joke.

"No," James said firmly. "There is nothing wrong with the Lemon Drop."

"I have been in your car."

James' expression hardened. "It's a perfectly good vehicle."

Gabe wanted to open his mouth to argue, but the ice below him was still too thin. He was tempted to have a cousin steal James' car so he could "help" James get a new one. It was so many miles past its use-by date; he thought of it as automotive botulism, and it was probably just as lethal. He moved his jaw a few times while James' hard look did not let up.

"Fine. But when it dies, you better get a new one before I find out, or I'm getting you a hybrid with the best safety rating I can find." Gabe tried to make it sound like a joke again.

James' expression began to soften. He wasn't out of the doghouse yet, but at least he wasn't working his way further into it.

"I'll keep that in mind."

An uncomfortable silence enveloped them. Thankfully the waitress showed up with a plate of spring rolls before it got too bad.

"Dylan wants to know how the Russian deal is going."

Gabe had seldom been so grateful for an obvious subject change. "I'm sure he does. If he ever decides to go into business, I'd be very scared. I think he's got the brain for it."

"He's always been smart. He started kindergarten in the bluebird reading group." James gave a proud little nod.

"That's good, I take it?"

"He already knew his alphabet and could count to twenty. He could even tie his shoes."

"Very impressive."

"And the first week, he got in trouble for getting a first-grade girl to kiss him in exchange for a ladybug he'd caught."

Gabe put his face into his hand, trying not to laugh. "You are really lucky you're not a grandparent yet, aren't you?"

James let out a long and long-suffering sigh. "You have no idea."

DYLAN HEAPED a slice of meatloaf onto his plate before passing the tray to James. James had tried to duplicate his mother's meatloaf recipe many times over the years, but never got it quite right. He was convinced she left out something when she passed him the recipe. He took his own helping before passing the tray back to his mother.

"James," his father started. "When do we get to meet this boyfriend of yours?"

James' fork froze halfway to his mouth. "Never" was the first answer to come into his mind. But not for any easily identifiable reason. He and Gabe were on better footing after their last dinner—not perfect, but better. He was a good guy, certainly nothing to be embarrassed about, and the entire Bay Area, to say nothing of vast portions of the business and computer world, knew they were dating.

"Um…. He's kind of in the middle of some complicated international business negotiations right now." His father gave James a stern look that made him feel like a teenager again. "I'll ask him about it, but he is really busy right now."

"And what does he do again?" his mother asked.

James glanced at Dylan. He'd assumed Dylan had already told his grandparents every little detail about who Gabe was and with great glee, but Dylan shook his head.

"He's an executive for TechPrim," James half mumbled.

Dylan snorted. "He's the *CFO* of TechPrim."

James felt the eyes of both his parents drilling into him. He curled himself over his meatloaf and shoved a large forkful into his mouth.

"The CFO?" his mother repeated.

James chewed slowly as a delay tactic.

"His name's Gabriel Juarez," Dylan supplied. "And he's the CFO and one of the founders."

He gave Dylan a sharp look. *Traitor*, he thought toward his son. Dylan grinned at him.

"I see," James' mother said without emotion.

James swallowed as his cheeks began to burn. "You know I can still ground you, right?" he muttered in Dylan's direction.

He'd managed to pull himself together and fake a good mood well enough that Dylan hadn't been aware of the falling-out with Gabe.

Dylan didn't stop grinning. "Hey, Dad, what time is it?"

Without thinking James checked the time on his phone. His incredibly fancy, top-of-the-line, so amazingly cool it automatically set the timer on your Wi-Fi-enabled coffeepot so the coffee was dripping no matter what time you set your wake-up alarm for, phone. His father simply raised an eyebrow upon seeing it.

"There was a recall on my old phone because it didn't handle humidity well." James shoved it back in his pocket.

"When do we get to check this guy over?"

James sighed and reminded himself that he was thirty-two and not a teenager. He squared his shoulders. "He's currently in the middle of working out a multibillion-dollar deal with a bunch of Russians. He's on conference calls at two in the morning on top of all his regular work. I will ask him about his schedule." In his heart James knew that Gabe would be willing to shift around his schedule, but he couldn't help but feel jealous of the time he got with Gabe, knowing how valuable it was. He also didn't want Gabe to feel like he was trying to push the relationship forward too fast, especially after he'd been the one to grind it to a halt. Not that James had any idea how fast things were supposed to be moving.

"Don't worry, Grandpa, I'm keeping an eye on Dad, and I'll drag Gabe in for inspection if I have to."

5

Gabe had been the one to suggest a quiet night in. He had cooked for James, nothing extravagant, had a glass of wine each. They'd watched *Young Frankenstein* and laughed at the same moments. They began to kiss during the credits, and Gabe had suggested they share a bath.

Now James had the feeling he was on the edge of a full-blown addiction to Gabe's bathtub, especially with Gabe in it. He could stretch his legs without touching the end, and he was sure, somehow, the water felt softer.

Gabe had one arm wrapped around him as he tilted his head back, leaning it against Gabe's shoulder. Gabe's free hand teased his cock and balls with careful strokes.

James had tried to keep still but couldn't hold it much longer. His hips jumped, hoping for a firmer touch. They hadn't had sex since James had walked out of that restaurant a few weeks earlier. Gabe hadn't pushed, as James had felt slightly off balance and unsure even after Gabe's apology and James' acceptance. Gabe ran his thumb around the tip of James' cock, and he felt far surer.

Gabe let go. "Roll over," he whispered in James' ear.

He turned over easily in the spacious tub and settled his head back on Gabe's shoulder, his lips at Gabe's neck. Gabe cupped his ass for a moment, then slowly eased just one finger between his cheeks. James hummed and snuggled closer. Gabe liked to play with his ass every time they took a shower or a bath. He didn't jump out of his skin like he did the first time, but Gabe hadn't gone past the single finger. A finger, slick with waterproof lube, slipped in.

They hadn't talked about it, but it had been building for a while, and James had a feeling that Gabe wanted to try to ease him a little further than one finger tonight. He had thought long and hard about it. He'd tried to imagine what it might feel like. He'd read that there were amazing moments of unbelievable pleasure. He'd also read that it was painful, uncomfortable, and pointless. Gabe did seem to fly apart whenever James pushed into him. His back would arch and he would beg for James to go harder and faster.

He relaxed as Gabe slowly worked that one finger in and out. He decided at the end of the day that if it was too much, he could simply say stop, and he was sure Gabe would stop, no matter what.

"Take a breath," Gabe whispered.

James did as told, and just as his lungs were filled, Gabe slid a second finger in. There was a bit of pain, a little burn, but the lust that shot through him in the same moment drowned all that out. He moaned, and his body shook. He pressed his cock hard into Gabe's thigh, looking for some friction.

"I love hearing you make that noise." Gabe slowly worked his fingers in and out while twisting them. "I love all your noises. Your moans and sighs and screams. Do you like it when I make you moan?"

James nodded, his ability to speak already shorting out. He shamelessly rubbed himself against Gabe's thigh, the water making it hard to build up heat. Gabe kissed his ear. "I think about this a dozen times every day. You in this tub, hard against me." Gabe gave a quick twist of his fingers. "Me, making your breath catch just before you whimper."

Gabe twisted his head around so James could look into those dark eyes. He felt that hard squeeze in his chest again. He was starting to develop a theory about what it meant, but it scared him as much as all the things Gabe could give him. He told himself it was just the lust of the moment. Gabe kissed him softly, then leaned his face against James', all the while still sliding his fingers in and out of James' body.

Then Gabe curled his fingers and hit just the right spot. James jumped and squeezed his eyes shut, even as he squeezed down around Gabe's fingers. Gabe stroked at that spot, and he felt his lungs begin to burn as his breath became fast and hard. He ground down on Gabe's thigh, sending water sloshing over the sides.

"That's right. I want to hear you cum for me." Gabe's fingers were working faster, driving in hard. Suddenly there was an extra burn. A tiny detached part of James' brain told him that Gabe must have slid in a third thick finger. He rocked forward hard, biting down on Gabe's shoulder. Gabe cried out and twisted his fingers around.

James pressed forward, a bellow escaping his lungs as he drained himself into the water.

He fought for breath, eyes still squeezed shut, his body aching from the force of it all. He could still feel Gabe hard against his hip as Gabe stroked his head. He opened his eyes and took in the rough bite mark on Gabe's shoulder.

"I'm sorry," James mumbled.

"Don't be."

"I meant about your shoulder."

"So did I." Gabe kissed his face. "Was I too rough on you?"

"No."

"Good." Gabe kissed him again. "Think you can get to the bed?"

James did a quick mental once-over of his body. He ached in strange and wonderful ways, and his limbs felt weak, but he was pretty sure he could stand. "I think I can manage."

"Good." Gabe stood and rinsed off the both of them before making a break for the bed. He curled against James, staring at him.

"Why are you looking at me like that?" James asked.

"Because I like looking at you."

"That's so weird."

"Weird that I want to look at my boyfriend? That I want to memorize every inch of his postorgasm blissed-out face so I can bring it out fifty times a day and just think about how gorgeous he looks to me?"

James felt that squeeze and for a half second thought he might cry. He took a deep breath instead. Even that was proving hard. "You are completely insane."

Gabe smiled. "Possibly, yes. But I think I make it work." Then Gabe was on him, pinning him to the bed, kissing him, enveloping his body as if he could somehow take James completely into himself. James ran his hands along Gabe's spine, then tangled them into his hair. He had noticed that if he pulled lightly on Gabe's hair he started to come undone. Gabe tilted his head back and ground his cock down against James.

He ran his fingers across the bite mark. Even in the pleasantly dim light of the bedroom, he could make out the impression of his own teeth. He ran his hand down over Gabe's shoulder until he could feel the rough scars left by road gravel and safety glass, minor injuries considering the speed at which Gabe flipped his car years before they ever met. He briefly considered where he'd be that night if Gabe's luck hadn't held. Almost certainly at home with a trashy book and a cup of cheap tea. Instead he was laid out on fine sheets while Gabe looked at him with unflinching desire. He could still feel the stretch where Gabe's fingers had twisted around and the pleasure of it was still fresh in his mind.

"If you want…," James whispered, then cleared his throat. "If you want more. I'm…." James swallowed hard but hoped the expression on his face might convey the words he couldn't quite get out.

Gabe kissed him. "Thank you. For tonight, I just want this. My body against yours. Is that okay?"

James nodded. He hadn't recharged yet, but he was still losing himself in the feel of Gabe's smooth skin and warm scent.

He set one hand to Gabe's backside, pulling him in close, and twisted the other carefully back into Gabe's curls. He thrust harder, working up the friction between them. James tugged; Gabe groaned. The bite mark caught his eye again. He put his lips to it and carefully sucked.

Gabe cried out and shuddered while James felt splashing across his body.

Gabe managed to collapse onto the bed instead of onto James. He gave a funny little giggle, then closed his eyes. James got up and retrieved a washcloth, hanging up the damp bath towels as he went.

When he returned, Gabe blinked sleepily at him, a soft smile on his face. He looked younger, even with the few strands of silver at his temple. James cleaned them both up without a word, then dropped the cloth into the hamper. When he got back to the bedroom, he found Gabe had crawled under the blankets. James joined him and was pulled close. He let the sound of Gabe's breathing lull him to sleep.

GABE only half dozed while James slept. James was prone to

taking little naps after sex. Not terribly long ones—thirty minutes, sometimes up to an hour if it was the end of a long day or week. He never begrudged James a moment of sleep. Gabe's doctor liked to regularly remind him how stress can render even a full night's sleep useless, not that he got many of those. If he wasn't dealing with problems on the other side of the planet, he just had good old-fashioned insomnia, nights where his brain wouldn't shut down, and he stared at the clock, feeling the seconds drag. He was sure James was in worse shape. He had a bet with himself that if he could ever get James off on a proper vacation he would spend the first few days doing nothing but sleeping.

He kissed the top of James' head. He'd managed to hide his amazement when James offered himself up like that. He had desperately wanted to say yes, to slide into James and watch his face as he broke apart. But Gabe was the partner who had been around the block a few times and had to be the responsible one. James wasn't ready for that, yet.

But that he'd offered…. Gabe felt himself trying to twitch toward life again. He let his mind roll around his new favorite/frustrating fantasies filed under the heading of "Things I Would Do For/With James if James Would Let Me." He knew a particular men's store in London that Gabe would love to clear out, having now gotten a brief close-up look at James' wardrobe. Of course James would hate it and resent being used as a living doll a hundred times worse than Gabe's own squirming discomfort at his first item of clothing that cost more than twenty dollars.

Gabe snorted. Twenty dollars seemed like nothing now, and if the last few deals fell into place…. It wasn't the money, though. Gabe had a stupid amount of money already. It was about changing the world and cementing TechPrim, the stupid little tech company with the typo in its name, into history.

He carefully rubbed his shoulder. He had never been a

masochist, a little hair pulling aside, but sweet, mild-mannered James sinking in his teeth like that had taken him to a whole special place. Knowing that he would be walking around with evidence of James on his body for at least a week was going to be very distracting. Not that he minded. Other boyfriends had tried marking him in the past, like they were claiming territory. Those boyfriends got tossed out of bed. Not James, though. He wasn't "other boyfriends."

James hummed and opened his eyes. "What are you thinking about?" he half mumbled.

"Not much, just a bit of free-form thought flow."

"Don't believe you."

"Thinking about how sexy you are when you let yourself let go."

James lowered his eyes. "What else are you thinking about? It can't all be about me."

"Thinking about work, a little. Thinking about all the things I'm going to need to do to get the ball rolling on certain plans. Thinking about this place I know in New York that makes amazing donuts."

"That's a lot of thoughts."

Gabe ran his fingers through James' hair. James pressed into his hand as if he was about to start purring. Gabe did have a lot of thoughts, and too many were swimming around alone, unvoiced, and disconnected. "I haven't told the guys about the company I just bought off Simon. Only Tamyra knows, and I didn't tell her about it in advance."

"You told me." James' voice was still soft and sleepy.

"I had to tell someone. It's too good not to. And besides, I don't think you're going to swoop in and try to buy the patents out from under me."

"No. Probably not."

He pulled James in close. It felt strange to put voice to ideas and plans that for so long had existed nowhere but inside his own head. But they were clamoring to be freed. "Do you know what rare earth minerals are?"

"Minerals that are rare?"

Gabe chuckled. "Basically, yeah. But they're used in a lot of modern technology. Flat-screen TVs, cell phones, things like that. Wouldn't be so much of a problem except the Chinese are sitting on about 97 percent of the world's deposits, and for a bunch of Communists, they're not big on sharing."

"And it means they're able to make devices using the elements cheaper than other countries and keep the export price up on the raw materials."

"I knew Dylan got his business sense from somewhere."

"Not a hard concept."

"No. Some new deposits have been found recently that look really good, except they're in places like Afghanistan and Pakistan and other places ending in 'stan.'"

James tilted his head an inch to the left. "But if you *could* get to them or some other new deposits, dig them up, and process them by yourself, then TechPrim could circumvent the Chinese, cut a huge amount of money off the manufacturing overhead, undercut prices on its competitors, sell the leftovers at higher prices to cover the mining costs, and get major public relations bonus points by putting manufacturing jobs back in developed countries where most of your products are still sold. And that is why you're buying up a lot of little companies that seem really random."

The speed at which James put it all together surprised Gabe, but he chastised himself for that surprise. Despite a lack of experience in the business world, James was no idiot. He slid his hand down James' spine, resting it at the small of his back.

"What did you want to be when you grew up? Before Dylan came along."

"I'm not sure. Either an astronaut or a museum curator. I

liked the idea of deciding where the dinosaurs should go or the paintings should hang."

"Was high-powered business mogul anywhere on your list?"

"Not that I can recall."

"Too bad. Most people wouldn't have strung all that together that fast. I mean, it's a little more complicated than that, but that's the rough outline."

James gave a little shrug as was his habit when faced with any praise. "It's not rocket science."

Gabe twisted to put a peck of a kiss on his lips. "You'd be surprised. Anyway, a poor bastard of a Russian who was basically trying to be TechPrim but with alcoholic business partners and an embezzler for a son, managed to have a similar idea and found some good deposits in a *slightly* more stable area than Afghanistan. Right now he's squatting on a shitload of europium, indium, neodymium, vanadium, and a bunch of other stuff that he can't afford to dig up himself and doesn't want to leave to his son when he dies of lung cancer in a year."

"That's why he's selling."

"And that is why he's selling. He wants to make as much as possible and dump it into an account for his illegitimate daughter and grandchildren. He also wants to make sure his employees are taken care of. I can respect that."

James cast his gaze up for a moment, obviously thinking. "I'll guess that Solar Flare's patents have something to do with all these elements."

"Ah, yes, that, that is the big thick layer of icing on my cake." He snuggled in closer to James, relaxing against his body. "Do you know what the big problem with solar cells are?"

"They need the sun."

"Pretty much. And when do people use the most electricity?"

"At night."

"And when you go to charge standard batteries with

standard cells, a lot of power is lost, even more so when you're talking low voltage power, which is what most solar cells produce. So having a few around LA is fine, but it's hardly worth the investment once you get to Seattle."

James grinned. "Let me guess, Solar Flare has patents for efficient solar cells."

"And more importantly a gizmo that charges batteries with minimal power loss. Now let me send you to business school, please?"

James made a face like he had a bad taste in his mouth. "Thank you, no. But they have solar cells?"

"Revolutionary ones."

"And they need these rare earth elements."

"Oh yes. They've got a prototype for a set of panels and batteries that would allow the average homeowner to go completely off mains for a minimum eight months out of the year anywhere south of Toronto and north of Invercargill. They would cost about as much as a dishwasher to buy and install, and the panels are half the size of current ones on the market. Full return on investment in two years or less. With a couple extra panels, you could charge up an electric car for the day." Gabe couldn't keep the excitement out of his voice. "*But* they need stacks of indium, and the best batteries for them need plenty of vanadium."

"Which you are about to get cheap, or cheaper, assuming the Russia deal goes through, allowing you to make solar panels at a price attractive to middle America."

Gabe rolled onto his back and spread his arms wide toward the heavens. "Bingo. I mean, it won't get us off foreign oil or solve the energy crisis—"

"But it'll normalize it. Take it out of the purview of hippies. People already have TechPrim computers, phones, entertainment systems, their cars decked out in TechPrim stuff. Why not TechPrim solar panels?"

"And even if I can't manage to sell it here, Germany is 30 percent solar already. They'll snap it all up."

James rolled over to look Gabe in the eyes. "And no one knows about this?"

"About the Solar Flare bit, it's just you, me, and Tamyra. Am I crazy for trying this?"

James didn't answer right away. Instead he flung his leg over Gabe's body, straddling his hips. "No. It makes sense."

"Oh thank God." The relief that flooded him with those few words was staggering in a way Gabe had never imagined. He sat up and pressed his lips to James', hard, before flopping back down. "When you sit on your own idea long enough, you start wondering if maybe you're delusional."

"It's going to piss off a lot of people."

"I know." A giggle sounding more than a little manic bubbled its way from Gabe. "It'll be a toss-up as to who puts out the first hit, China, OPEC, PG&E, or Simon, when he realizes what he's given up over a game of golf." He settled his hands on James' hips, where his skin happened to be particularly smooth.

"Why did you tell me all that?"

"Because I *really* needed to tell someone. Someone I can trust. I've been sitting on it for too damn long and have been starting to wonder if I'm crazy."

"You have Tamyra or Nate or Frank."

"I know, but they're... they'd want to talk about practicalities, supply chains, business plans. I needed to tell someone who might understand what I'm hoping to do."

James leaned over and kissed him softly. "You're trying to change the world."

Gabe brushed their lips together. "Yes," he replied softly.

James smiled at him. "I won't tell anyone. Even Dylan."

"He'd probably want in on it. And I know you won't. It's one of the many things I really like about you. You're not working an angle on me or out to stab anyone in the back. Your first thought isn't 'How can I use this to my advantage?.'"

"You seem to know me well."

Gabe rolled quickly, toppling James off him and switching their positions. He ran his hands across James' chest, thumbing his nipples, fluttering his eyes shut. "Oh, there is a lot I still don't know. I'm sure there are vast depths to you. But I like to think I've got a handle on the basics. I like to think I'm right when I came to the conclusion that you are the very rarest of things, and that is a good man."

James glanced away. "You keep saying things like that."

"Like what? That I think you're good, rare, special?"

James shifted slightly away in discomfort. "I'm really not. I'm just one of the masses."

"No." He brushed his fingers across James' cheek and down to his lips.

James kissed them. "You've been chewing on your fingers again. You should try putting vanilla extract on them. Or chili oil."

"See, I've been doing that for years, and not a single other boyfriend has ever commented except to tell me it was gross. They never tried to help me stop." James laced their fingers together. "Maybe you need to sleep next to me every night, holding my hands so I don't chew on them in my sleep."

"I think that may become a difficult commute for one of us."

Quit your crappy job! Gabe screamed in his head. *Move in with me; go back to college; learn the best place to put dinosaurs! Let me give you what you deserve just for being a decent person!*

Gabe brushed his lips across James' knuckles. "How about we start with tonight?"

"I think I can do tonight."

STEAM ROLLED from Mrs. Gonzales's kitchen, making the air thick. James rolled another tamale and added it to a steadily growing stack. Gabe had dropped him off, and by the time he'd gotten to his apartment door, he could smell the boiling chicken and onions filling the hall.

He changed out of the dark blue silk shirt he'd found for five bucks at Thrift Town before following his nose to Mrs. Gonzales's door. The ladies had gotten quiet as he'd let himself in and grabbed a plate. That quiet meant he had been the main topic of gossip, for possibly the first time since moving in.

He rolled a few tamales before sighing. He had been hoping to spend the afternoon discussing some sudden plot shifts in *El Lamento del Cuervo*, but it looked like his love life was going to be a more interesting topic. "Adelante, preguntan lo que quieran."

"How rich is he?" Mrs. Valadez asked before anyone could start with something more tactful.

"I don't know. I haven't asked. It would be rude."

"Have you met his family yet?" Mrs. Serrano asked. She had the largest family in the building.

"No, not yet." That got some murmurs of disapproval.

"Are you moving in with him?"

"I haven't even met his family yet. I think that is getting ahead of things."

"You should meet his family," Mrs. Gonzales stated firmly.

"He's very busy. He's got a very important job. He has to work a lot."

Mrs. Gonzales shook her finger at him. "Those are all excuses. If he has some bad ones in his family, he needs to tell you now and introduce you to the rest." There were general nods of agreement.

"I'm sure he will."

"Is he good in bed?" Mrs. Silva asked. The other women

gave her hard looks. She was the dirty old lady of their little group. It was almost her job to ask that.

James gave a noncommittal shrug and tried to focus on his tamales, even as he heard some naughty giggles.

His phone started vibrating in his pocket. He wiped his fingers and quickly fished it out.

"Hello?"

"Hey, it's me." Gabe's voice seemed to echo in from a distance, and James could hear traffic in the background. "I just got a call from my sister, and apparently everyone's schedule has finally aligned, and the family is all getting together for dinner next Saturday. I was wondering if you'd like to join me?"

"To meet your family?"

The women who'd been watching all gave stern nods and hard eyes.

"Yeah, if you want. I mean, if you'd like to avoid them, I'd totally understand, or if you had other plans—"

"No, Saturday sounds fine."

"Good. I'll pick you up at seven?"

"Seven is fine."

"Good. I'll talk to you later."

"Okay."

"Bye."

James hung up the phone. "There, I'm meeting his family. ¿Feliz?"

6

James tried to smooth his shirt down. "You look fine," Gabe told him for about the fiftieth time. He hoped James wouldn't regret agreeing to meet his family. They could be a handful, but this was the first time his schedule had matched up with all three of his sisters' in ages.

He knocked on the front door of a tidy suburban home. He'd gotten it for his parents the year after TechPrim opened their first international office. He could have gotten it earlier and gotten a bigger one, but his father hadn't believed Gabe could afford it until *The Wall Street Journal* printed an article about Gabe and TechPrim.

The door opened, and Gabe was hit with the smell of boiling chicken.

"Hey, Uncle Gabe." Alisa, his eldest (and privately his favorite) niece, pulled him into a hug.

"Hey there, when did you get back to town?"

"This morning."

"James, this is my niece Alisa. She's been down in Mexico as part of a research project on indigenous language groups. Alisa, this is my boyfriend, James Maron."

"Nice to meet you." James shook her hand and didn't look too nervous. Alisa opening the door was a stroke of luck. It would give him the chance to ease James into his family before meeting his mother.

Alisa stepped aside, letting them in. Gabe took another sniff of the air. He identified boiled chicken, boiled pork, onion, and a hint of pepper, cut with a slightly starchy smell. "So, your grandmother's making tamales."

"About a billion of them. Come on. The assembly line is in the dining room."

In the dining room, the table was covered with bowls of shredded pork and chicken, masa paste, and damp corn husks, plus trays of assembled tamales. Gabe's sisters and father were sitting around the table, diligently assembling the little rolls for steaming. Everyone looked up at Gabe and James.

"Hey, everyone, this is James Maron, my boyfriend. James, this is my father, Emilio Juarez."

James immediately shook hands. "It's a pleasure to meet you, sir."

Gabe's father smiled. "And you."

"And these three are my sisters, Alandria, Rosalina, Nina."

"Hi." His sisters wiped masa paste off their fingers to shake his hand.

"And this." Gabe waved his arm grandly across the table. "Is the fine art of industrial-scale tamale making that my mother engages in on occasion. And since there is no such thing on earth as a small tamale recipe, this might take a while. I'm sorry, I thought we were just having dinner."

"It's not a problem." James had a slightly odd smile on his face that Gabe had never seen before. "Can I help out?"

Alandria, the eldest of the Juarez children, patted a seat beside her. "Of course." She handed James a plate to work on. "What you do is you take a corn husk, lay it flat. Then you take a bit of the masa." She dropped a spoonful of the thick paste onto the wet corn husk. "Try to spread it out even. Then some of the filling." She made a log of shredded chicken down the center. "Now you roll it very carefully, trying to keep everything inside the husk." That was the step that Gabe had never mastered, carefully rolling up the corn husk so nothing leaked out and it didn't totally disintegrate when steamed.

James nodded slowly with a look of concentration on his face. "Like this?" James took a corn husk and dropped it on his plate. Twenty seconds later, a perfectly rolled tamale sat on James' plate, and his hands were completely clean.

His sisters all looked at Gabe. Gabe shrugged. He had no idea where James picked up the ability to do that. They looked at James, who had already taken another corn husk. "The women in my building get together every other month and make about five billion tamales, and if I sit quietly, keep *out* of the kitchen, and help roll, then I get to take some home, which is a good thing because Dylan's been eating like a horse since he turned twelve." James completed another tamale, identical to the previous one in size and shape. "I have been doing this regularly for about twelve years now. Mrs. Silva, next door, does hers in banana leaves. Around Christmas she does turkey ones and makes me wrap them up like little presents for her. That gets tricky." James completed yet another, hardly even looking.

Alandria looked back up at Gabe. "I like him." James ducked his head, his cheeks going pink. "But you have to roll too."

Gabe shoved up his sleeves, wishing he'd worn something a little less nice. He'd never managed to roll tamales without getting at least one all over himself. He tried to eyeball James' technique, but his hands were moving too quickly. Gabe could hear clanging coming from the kitchen. His mother mastered her own steaming technique and usually kicked everyone out of the kitchen to take care of that part herself. Soon she would emerge, however, and the tricky introduction would happen. The rest of the family didn't care about his sexuality, or if they did, he'd bought their acceptance by sending their kids to private schools and paying for their doctors and lawyers.

His mother, on the other hand, had learned to be polite, but that was about it. His father playing mediator kept the tenuous peace between the two of them. Even with that, they'd spent the last decade and then some keeping their conversations as neutral as possible.

Gabe brought his mind back to the present. James had produced a neat little stack while Gabe was still trying to smooth out masa for his first tamale.

"James," Alandria started. "Gabe never tells us anything about the people he's seeing. So you're going to have to."

"I do—" Gabe tried to object, but Alandria just waved a hand in his general direction.

"Um… I'm a team manager for Technical Services at UCB. I have a son, Dylan, who is almost eighteen and is likely to be the death of me, and despite what Gabe might say, I am possibly one of the most boring people you are ever going to meet."

"You roll tamales well," Alisa pointed out.

"After the first few thousand, I sort of got the hang of it." Everyone at the table chuckled. They knew James was not exaggerating. Most of the recipes Gabe had seen for tamales started with "Take two whole chickens and an equal weight of pork." And those were single-family recipes. Enough to satisfy an entire building would easily take out a small farm's worth of animals.

"James, how did you meet our Gabriel?" his father asked.

"He was a guest lecturer at UCB, and his computer froze up. I unfroze it, and he was good enough to buy me a cup of coffee. Which I have to say is something no other guest lecturer or even professor has ever done. That got my attention."

The kitchen door opened, and everyone looked up. Gabe's

mother was in her plain, faded yellow apron. A light sheen of sweat decorated her face from standing over gallons of boiling water. She held a large empty tray. Gabe hadn't seen her in a while, and there was always a moment of shock, the way she looked so much older than in his memory. In his mind she still had soft black hair like his, not the dark steel gray it had become.

"Mom, this is James, my boyfriend," Gabe said carefully. He had only ever gotten as far as introducing a few of his boyfriends to his mother, whereas his father had met several of them and even gotten along with a couple. "James, this is my mother, Adela Juarez."

James stood and held out his hand. "It's very nice to meet you, ma'am."

She gave James' hand a perfunctory shake, then looked at the tidy stack of tamales in front of James' plate. "You made those?"

"Yes, ma'am."

His mother looked at them for a few more seconds before nodding and gathering them up onto the empty tray with the rest for steaming. Once she was back in the kitchen, James sat down, and everyone breathed.

"Well now, that should be the worst of it," Gabe said with a sigh. It was far and away the easiest introduction between his mother and a boyfriend. Then again, he'd never brought home a boyfriend who could assemble perfect tamales.

Gabe looked at the half-finished one sitting on his plate and tried to roll it. James looked over just in time to see the masa start to squeeze through.

"Hold on." James stopped his hands. "You overfilled it." He unrolled it, scraped at it with a spoon, then rerolled it, setting it with the rest.

"You're just trying to make me look bad."

"Leave him alone, Gabe," Alandria scolded. "He's the first

one you've brought home who knows what the hell a tamale is."

"He also watches the novelas."

"There's nothing wrong with that," James stated in his own defense.

"Which ones?" Nina asked. She was a connoisseur. Gabe had spent large portions of his teenaged years fighting with her for control of the TV. He usually lost.

"Right now? *El sueño del corazón*, *Siete palomas*, *Tres corazones de fuego*, and I just started *El lamento del cuervo*."

Alandria turned to her brother. "Gabe, keep this one."

"What do you think is up with Father Joseph on *El lamento del Cuervo*?" Nina asked James.

"Murderer on the run. Obviously."

Gabe and Alisa exchanged looks and rolled their eyes as the conversation shifted to convoluted romances, back-stabbing illegitimate children, greedy landlords, and pious virgins. The conversation started to shift in and out of Spanish and, much to Gabe's embarrassment, he was having a hard time keeping up with it. James, however, was speaking a mile a minute, and his hands were, if anything, speeding up. His mother stepped from the kitchen with an empty tray while James was in the middle of a complicated explanation about where a novice nun fit into an attempt to steal a cattle ranch. At least, that's what Gabe thought the conversation was about. His mother listened for a few moments. She was as hooked on the novelas as Nina, which was why Gabe usually lost his battles for the television.

"Rosa will never give up her vows," his mother stated with certainty.

James shook his head. "She will if Renaldo tries to sell off the ranch, because it was her father's dying wish that the ranch stay in the family, and she is the only one who can lawfully claim it."

Gabe was proud. It was about a ranch.

His mother squinted at James for a few seconds. "But Eduardo may kill Renaldo before it gets that far."

James thought for a second, then shrugged. "Maybe, but I don't think he has the... guts to do it in the end."

His mother tipped her head in half agreement before gathering up another tray and retreating back to the kitchen.

Alandria patted James on the hand. "It's official, she likes you more than any other of Gabe's boyfriends. Possibly combined."

James ducked his head, but Gabe could see him trying to fight down a shy smile. He gave James a little nudge with his shoulder. James just kept rolling tamales, trying not to grin.

The conversation started to flit around between his sisters and Alisa again, with Gabe just listening quietly. Alandria was right; his mother seemed to have taken to James better than anyone else he'd ever been brave enough to bring home. With that bit of revelation, Gabe started to relax and even enjoy himself. Some of his fonder memories of childhood were sitting around his grandmother's table with his sisters, helping to roll tamales or peel the skin off chilies so she could can them. It was only when they all grew up, when his sisters started having babies and he went off to college and started dating men, that a tension began to permeate family gatherings. But apparently James' encyclopedic and esoteric knowledge of a decade of telenovelas seemed to be washing that tension right away. If only someone had told him that years ago.

The last of the corn husks were filled in record time, thanks in no small part to James' expert skills, before Gabe's mother came back out, gathered up the rest, and ordered them to clean up and set the table for dinner.

Dinner went surprisingly smooth, with Alisa dominating the conversation with stories of her travels, people she'd met, scrapes she'd gotten into, and how she was going to leverage it all into a PhD and teaching job. And that was why she was secretly Gabe's favorite. She could have fallen into the same pattern of mediocrity, second-rate jobs, and abandoned education like a lot of his extended family. Instead she was determined to see the world and learn as much as she could. In between her stories, James was subtly grilled on his job and family, but seemed to come through it with general approval.

It was only after dinner that Gabe and James were quietly separated, James getting swept up by his sisters while Gabe was herded off by his father. James sent him an understanding smile.

"I need your help with something in the garage," Gabe's father said, ushering him toward the door.

"Sure." The garage was dark and cool. "What do you need help with?"

His father reached behind a toolbox and pulled out a bottle of mescal about three quarters full with a handwritten label. It looked positively toxic. "Drinking this before your mother finds it."

"Oh, God, Dad." His father pulled out two water glasses from behind the toolbox and filled them with the sickly golden liquid. It was nearly enough to empty the bottle. Obviously refusing was not going to be an option.

Gabe took a glass and took a sip. He forced back a cough at the sharp burn, while his father took a large swallow of his. Gabe took another sip but didn't comment. He wasn't sure if his dad wanted to talk or drink or do both, but he knew better than to make assumptions.

His father took another couple of sips, not even wincing. "I like James. You should keep him."

"Thank you, Dad. I like him too."

"No. I mean it. The other men you've brought home have been children. Even the ones older than you, you could tell they just wanted to play. This one, he already has a family, he understands responsibility, priorities, he could keep you in line."

Gabe felt the mescal start to go to his head. "I wish he'd play more. He's got too much responsibility already. He needs to have a bit of fun once in a while."

"I'm sure he will manage. But he also makes you happy. I can tell."

Gabe nodded and took a few more sips. "He does." When there was a space in both glasses, his father emptied the rest of the bottle into them.

"And how is your work?"

Gabe gave a small shrug. It was a complicated question at the best of times. Even when things were going perfectly, Gabe felt like they were teetering on the edge of disaster. "Busy. Got a lot of stuff going on."

"Thinking up new ways of becoming richer."

"That's not my motivation, and you know it."

"Yes."

"But I am going to change the world, Dad. Some rich people are going to hate me for some of the things I'm going to do, but I'm going to make the world a better place. You'll be able to point to some amazing things and say, 'I know who made that happen.'"

"I'm always pointing to things and telling people that my son is responsible for it. People don't believe me, but I tell them anyway."

Gabe took a large swallow of mescal, his throat having been numbed to the worst of the burn. "Thank you."

"For what?"

"Admitting I'm your son."

"Why wouldn't I?"

Gabe twitched his shoulders in a small shrug. He didn't want to say the obvious answer out loud.

"I always knew, you know," his father continued. "Right

from the time you were small. I tried to tell your mother, but she wouldn't hear of it. No son of hers would be that way."

Gabe nearly choked on a mouthful of mescal. His father had never once mentioned his sexuality, even in passing, except to approve or disapprove of his boyfriends. "I didn't know that."

"She tried to send *me* to a priest for even saying such things. And what would a priest do, tell me that my son was wrong or broken? My Gabriel. What the hell do they know about it?"

"They say they speak for God," Gabe muttered into his glass.

His father waved at him dismissively. "I do not trust any man who will not speak for himself, and that includes God." Gabe broke out laughing. "But don't tell your mother I said that."

"I will take it to my grave, I promise."

His father patted his cheek. "You're a good boy. Now drink that. I have another half bottle I need to get rid of before your mother tries to clean up out here."

Gabe groaned but tipped his head back and took another swallow. They drank in companionable silence and were into the second bottle when the door to the garage opened. Gabe shielded his eyes from the light where James and two of his sisters stood with their lips pinched and their arms folded.

"I take it I'm driving tonight?" James said.

"I'll get us a cab." Gabe was aware of the slur in his voice and the fact that his lips were feeling numb. He tried to lick them but couldn't quite tell what his tongue was doing. He looked down at the last two inches of mescal in his glass and chugged it just as his mother joined James at the door. He watched his father empty his own glass in one swallow.

His mother shook her finger. "Do not come crying to me in the morning when you are sick."

"Mescal doesn't make you sick in the mornings. Everyone knows that," Gabe's father stated with certainty.

Bullshit, Gabe thought, fully aware of the epic hangover looming on the horizon. His mother marched in, took his father by the arm, and marched back out with him. He looked up at James.

"Come on. I'll drive. Dylan's got his last game in the morning, and you look like you're about to pass out."

"I'm fine. Really."

———

GABE WAS NOT unfamiliar with the sensation of waking up completely hungover, but it had been a long time since he'd done it in a bed so small. He had some vague memories of James dumping him into bed, but James was nowhere to be seen, and he was sprawled across what little bed there was.

He heard a shower turn on at the same moment his stomach decided to voice an objection to the previous night's activities. He sprinted for the bathroom, only marginally aware that he was in just his shorts. By some luck the bathroom door was unlocked, and he stumbled in just in time to be sick. He heard the shower curtain pulled back, but he didn't dare raise his head from its position half-buried in the toilet.

"Um…. Gabe?"

Gabe had been hoping it was James and not Dylan in the shower. "Yes, Dylan."

"Are you okay?"

"Be very thankful your father's idea of father/son quality time does not involve drinking a bottle and a half of bootleg mescal."

"Ah, I see. Would you mind not flushing until I get the soap out of my hair?"

"No problem." Dylan yanked the shower curtain back into place. Gabe still hadn't moved as he tried to will his body back into some semblance of control. Dylan must have rushed his shower because just a couple minutes later it was turned off. He still didn't move, not yet trusting his stomach.

There was the sound of a tap running before a plastic cup was pressed into his hand. "Drink that, then take a shower yourself. There are painkillers in the medicine chest, and Dad is making oatmeal."

"Thank you," Gabe croaked.

He heard Dylan chuckle and leave. Gabe slowly pushed himself up and followed Dylan's advice. By the time he found his clothes neatly folded on top of James' dresser, he was past the "praying for death" phase of a really solid hangover. Now he was in the "still wouldn't mind death, but would rather just go back to sleep" phase.

He made his way into the kitchen, bowed by the crushing embarrassment. It was one thing to have a few glasses of wine and crash at your boyfriend's place; it was another thing to get fairly shitfaced, steal his bed, then get sick in his bathroom in front of his teenaged son. James was wrapped in a blue, faded, threadbare bathrobe, his hair still disheveled from sleep.

"Morning." He tried to sound far perkier than he felt.

"Hey there. How are you feeling?"

"I've felt better."

James motioned him to one of the empty seats at the table. Dylan was already into a bowl of oatmeal, a plate of eggs, and a banana. "Please tell me I didn't kick you out of your bed last night?" Gabe's voice came out sounding close to tears, but that was possibly the hangover as much as for remorse for what he had done. Things had been going so well with James he was desperately hoping that two bottles of mescal hadn't ruined things again.

"No. I managed to shove you over."

"I am *really* sorry. I mean really, really sorry. I had no idea my dad wanted to drink with me."

"It's okay." James didn't sound too mad, or even particularly irritated. If anything he looked amused. That could only mean one thing. Gabe braced himself.

"Okay, what did I do last night?"

James bit his lower lip for a second. "Nothing, really. Mostly you just kept trying to sing 'Hotel California' in Spanish. Except either your Spanish is really bad or you couldn't actually remember any of the lyrics."

Gabe pressed his face into his hand as James finally broke and started to giggle. "Think you can handle some oatmeal?"

Gabe's stomach said no while his brain pointed out that it might be settling. "I'll try some."

James put a glass of water and a bowl in front of him. It held something beige and pasty, and there were some raisins on top, but the smell was appealing. "I'm going to grab my own shower."

"I'll be here."

James put a kiss on the top of his head while still giggling as Gabe took a bite. Gabe waited until he heard the shower running before slowly collapsing forward, pressing his face to the table. While there he sent up a thanks to anything that might be listening that James was the forgiving type.

Dylan laughed. "Still not feeling great?"

He was tempted to give Dylan the finger, but that would involve moving. "I've had worse hangovers; dangers of international business. You're expected to drink whatever the locals pour and keep up with them. Matter of honor. Except in India. I love doing deals in India. The weddings take four hours but no one expects you to drink."

"That's good to know." He could hear the laughter under Dylan's words.

"The first time I met your father I was still hungover from closing a big deal in Japan. Spent the whole flight praying for death." He pushed himself up and managed to shove another spoonful of oatmeal into his mouth. It did feel nice in his stomach, despite the vast quantities of energy needed to lift the spoon.

"Dad said he thinks meeting your family went well?"

Gabe nodded. "My sisters approved, my dad approved, and my mother didn't make any snide comments about hell, which is about as close to approval as she gets. I think your father's vast esoteric knowledge of the telenovelas helped smooth things there."

"I knew all that would come in handy for him one of these days." Dylan's phone pinged. He looked down and smiled.

"New girlfriend?"

"New old girlfriend. Maybe. She's looking for a rebound. Plus angling for a prom date."

Gabe wondered what his high school dating life would have been like if texting had been invented. Probably not that much different, he had to admit. He looked down at his to-do list on his phone. It had about three-dozen items on it, but one stood out.

"Dylan, can I ask you some advice?"

"Sure."

"What do women like?" Dylan raised an eyebrow. "Not like that. I need to get Tamyra something nice. She's been working for me almost ten years now, and I need to get her something as nice as possible, except she does basically all my shopping of that sort for me."

"Okay, I get the idea." Dylan finished off his eggs in two bites. "Any vague idea of what she might like?"

"I'm thinking jewelry, but I've drawn a blank anywhere past that." In truth, Gabe could barely think past the steady pounding behind his eyes.

"Jewelry is always good. Most women enjoy receiving that."

"So... I don't know, diamonds?"

Dylan waved his hand. "Boring. Diamonds are like roses.

Nice, expensive, but not original. You want her to think you put thought into this."

"I am putting thought into this. Hungover thought," Gabe admitted, "but it still counts."

"Okay. What does she usually wear, how does she dress?"

"Perfectly. I stumble off a twenty-hour flight looking dead, and she walks off the same flight looking like she just stepped out of the pages of a catalog."

"Can you give me a little more detail?"

Gabe brought up the pictures on his phone and flipped through them. He found the one of Tamyra with Sara and Christine, Frank and Nate's PAs, taken at a large industry conference before Christmas.

"Here." He handed the phone to Dylan and laid his head back on the table. "The TechPrim Angels. Tamyra's the one in the middle."

Dylan didn't say anything for several seconds, just looked at the picture. "Is she single?"

"Too old for you, and lesbian."

"What about the other two?"

"Too old for you and lesbians."

"All three of them?"

"Yep."

"Was that on purpose?"

Gabe grinned. "Officially and legally, no." Unofficially it had solved so many problems.

"Okay." Dylan stretched out the word before squinting closely at the picture. "This is sort of her usual wear?"

"Yeah."

"Okay, jewel tones, not too flashy. You'll want to go with something like emeralds or rubies. Single stones, necklace, earrings, matched stones, something like that." Dylan handed the phone back over.

"Rubies?"

"Expensive but not generic."

"Okay…." Gabe tried to properly engage his brain again. "Now where the fuck do I get ruby earrings?"

"If you were one of your VPs, I'd say the mall or something like that. But you're you and I'll bet she knows exactly how much you make, so you're going to have to go custom made. Find some high-end guy, get it designed, the whole thing."

"Without her finding out."

"That's *your* problem."

The shower turned off, and Gabe tried to answer a few of his messages. All he managed to do in the end was text Tamyra a quick note about his location and what physical state he was in. She texted back telling him not to reply to any important messages until he was less hungover. He decided to take that as permission to slack off.

He shoveled a few more bites of oatmeal into his mouth, then chugged the water. James came into the kitchen dressed, but his hair was still damp. Gabe had the urge to reach up and rumple it.

"Feeling better?" James asked.

"A bit."

Dylan glanced over at the clock. "Hey, we need to get going soon."

"You've got a game, right?"

"Last of the season."

"Mind if I tag along? Tamyra told me not to answer any important messages until I feel less hungover, which at this rate means I shouldn't be doing any work until at least six, maybe seven."

"Sure," Dylan said, moving his dishes to the sink. "The last game always has good crowds."

"Nervous?"

"Meh. We're enough games ahead that we could not show up and still get a pennant. We're just out to have fun today."

"And win?" Gabe added.

"Always."

The game wasn't quite as casual as Gabe had been led to believe. The Cougars might have had the whole series in the bag, but their competitors, the Mustangs, wanted to see them go out with a loss. Or at least some injuries. Gabe winced as a Mustang crashed into first base with more force than was strictly necessary, turning baseball into a full-contact sport. The Cougars retaliated by tagging the same player out at second via a ball/fist driven into his stomach. The crowd started to get ugly by the third inning.

"Does it get like this often?" Gabe whispered to James.

"Once in a while. It doesn't take much to get teenaged boys amped up. The coaches will try to calm them down between innings. In theory."

By the fifth, the score was tied, and the casualty count was rising. An "accidentally" bad pitch clipped one batter on the side of the head. Runs into home were starting to look like football tackles, to the terror of the poor catchers. Dylan was reasonably safe in the outfield, but every time he came up at bat, James' fingers dug into Gabe's knee. Gabe was sure he'd have bruises but didn't do anything to stop it.

There was a crack of the bat, and the ball arched high. Dylan broke into a sprint. The ball dropped into the edge of the outfield as Dylan rounded for second. There was a toss and the dull thud of the ball connecting with the second baseman's glove. Dylan slid, his bad ankle heading in first. Gabe winced as James' fingers dug in deep.

A small cloud of dust settled, and the umpire called safe. Dylan didn't get up right away, and James leapt to his feet with Gabe right behind, his heart in his throat. Then Dylan pried himself out of the dirt with just one foot. Gabe started to wonder if a summer would be enough to recover from orthopedic surgery, James' pride be damned. Dylan took a breath and put his other foot down. He stood for half a second before leading off to third. James sat back down, and Gabe took his hand, giving it what he hoped was a comforting squeeze.

Dylan was tagged out at third, and the inning was over after the next batter up bunted.

The game was still tied up in the ninth when Dylan got his last at bat. Gabe had been watching him in the outfield. He didn't seem to be limping or in any pain, but Gabe could recognize a good poker face a mile off. Dylan could be screaming inside without so much as a frown touching his face.

Dylan got pitched four junk balls that resulted in four fouls and a walk. It was a cheap move, but Gabe was quietly relieved that Dylan wouldn't be sliding into anything. The next kid up, a skinny little thing who hadn't done anything but bunt or get struck out, walked up to the plate. He swung at the first two balls for two easy strikes. He caught a piece of the next, sending the ball practically behind him. The pitcher smirked from the mound and tossed a ball that was nearly invisible with its speed. There was a crack. The ball sailed into the air and kept going. The outfielders jumped for it, but it landed just in front of the fence. The kid made it to second while two other players made it home. Gabe could see tears in the kid's eyes.

"That's the first time he's made it past first base all season," James said as the crowd cheered.

"Good for him."

"They only keep him around because he's a great shortstop."

The skinny kid was lifted by his teammates, still in tears, while the Cougars' fans took to the field.

James hugged his son, and Dylan lifted his dad right off the ground in return. Gabe offered a handshake and a slap on the back. A girl pushed her way through the crowd; she didn't look like the baseball type. Her short black hair was spiked and frosted with glossy dark blue tips that matched her blue eyeliner and knitted fingerless gloves. Gabe didn't know you could get eyeliner that shade of blue.

Dylan turned and saw her. "Catherine." He pulled her into a hug, and she hugged him back. "I didn't think you'd come."

"Like I'd miss your last game."

Gabe wondered if this was Catherine, the love of Dylan's life. Judging by the type of smile on his face, he was willing to bet yes.

"How's your ankle?" she asked.

"It's fine," Dylan answered a little too quickly.

"Hi, Catherine," James greeted.

"Hello, Mr. Maron."

"I hear you got into Boston U, congratulations."

"Thank you."

"Are you coming to the party?" Dylan asked, full of eager energy.

"Wouldn't miss it."

Dylan's smile got brighter, and Gabe felt a little pity. He'd spent time pining away for someone who just wanted to be a friend.

Gabe let himself and the niggling remains of his hangover be whisked along to the postseason party. Someone had booked a pizza place where each player seemed determined to eat an entire pizza on their own. Coach Frasier had some strict ideas and policies regarding athletes' nutrition that were rapidly going out the window.

Gabe nibbled his pizza, drank some full-sugar soda, and reminisced on his own high school days. Off in the corner, Dylan talked quietly to Catherine. The suave ladies' man player act was gone, and his body language spoke of a man tragically in love and more than a little desperate.

James sat down next to Gabe with another slice of pizza for himself. He spent a few minutes watching the little teenaged drama as well. "How long has Dylan been desperately in love with her?"

"Since he was seven. She lived down the hall from us with her mother for about six months while a divorce shook out. She was the first girl not to fall for his act."

"I can see how that would become love."

"It's one of the reasons I like her. They actually dated a couple of years ago, but she wanted to focus on her music."

Dylan picked up her hand in his.

"What's he doing now?"

"Trying to talk her into going with him to prom." Catherine rolled her eyes, tilting her whole head back in the process. "Not sure how well it's going."

Gabe wiped the pizza grease from his lips. Before getting sidetracked by alcohol the night before, there was something he'd been planning to ask James. Dylan's plight brought it back to mind.

"Actually there's been something I've been meaning to ask you."

"Yes."

"Um…. Every May, TechPrim throws itself a birthday party. The employees call it prom as sort of a joke. There are rented tuxes and formal dresses, a certain amount of lame dancing, and someone always gets drunk and tries to have sex in the bathroom. Anyway, I was wondering if you'd like to come with me this year?"

"You're inviting me to prom?" There was laughter in James' words.

"Basically, yeah."

James grinned. "Okay. Sure. I kind of missed prom the first time around. I don't have a tux, though."

"Don't worry. I can arrange something. I know people." In the far booth, Dylan suddenly grinned while Catherine rolled her eyes again, but she was also smiling. "That boy does know how to be persistent."

"That he does."

"So," James started as soon as he and Dylan got through the apartment door. "Taking Catherine to prom?"

"Technically we're going stag together because we're not together, and she doesn't really believe in social conventions like prom."

"You talked her into going to prom with you." Dylan took a bow. "You do know she's going to the other side of the country?" As much as James liked Catherine, she was the first and possibly only girl to truly break Dylan's heart.

"I know. And there will be other people there, and she'll probably hook up with someone and date and whatnot but...."

"Boston is a long way." He didn't want to hurt Dylan, but he was never sure if Dylan was fully in reality when it came to Catherine.

"I know, I know." Dylan's face fell, and he took a deep breath. "I know how this story ends. I do. I'm not an idiot. Can I just live in complete denial until she leaves in August? I mean, I know the odds and what's what but... denial? Please?"

"Sure." James gave his arm a small squeeze. "How's your ankle?"

"It's fine," Dylan answered. James gave him a hard look. Dylan was bad about underplaying injuries and seemed determined to give James a stress-related ulcer or aneurysm over it. "It's a little tender but not bad, and I've got some time to rest it up now, and I will. Promise."

"I just worry."

"I know, and I'm fine. Now how about you? You and Gabe looked like you were plotting something."

James allowed the change in subject. "Oh, that—apparently there's a company birthday party or something, and he wants me to go with him."

Dylan froze for a second. "The TechPrim prom? Of course you'd go, you're dating the CFO. Telling you this right now, Dad, it's kinda a big deal. TechPrim goes all out for these things. You're going to end up in the gossip columns again."

Gabe hadn't mentioned that, probably on purpose. James didn't like to back out of things he'd agreed to, and he was pretty sure Gabe had learned that about him as well.

He gave a little internal growl. "As long as my team doesn't forward it around campus, I'll live. And it might be nice if they spell my name correctly as well."

JAMES HIT SEND ON an e-mail that listed the weekend support problems and pointed out tactfully that hiring just one more person to do support on weekends would cut down on the amount of Monday morning that was spent answering angry messages and cranky e-mails.

He looked up at the pencils hanging over his head, then glanced down at his phone. It was a habit, checking for missed calls, despite the fact that his new phone would actually ring. Not that people called him all that often, but he was hoping to hear from Gabe. He wasn't expecting it, but he was hoping.

"Hey, Boss?"

"Yes, Dave?" James didn't even turn around.

"There are some guys at the front desk who want to see you."

James looked over his shoulder. "Who?"

Dave shrugged and gestured at the door. James would have chastised him about his message-taking abilities again, but for the past two days, he hadn't noticed a slick of Cheetos residue on any workstation or on Dave himself. He figured that earned Dave a couple of days' grace before starting in on his next bad habit.

At the front desk were a couple men in jeans and TechPrim polo shirts along with a couple of large boxes.

"James Maron?" one of the men asked.

"Yes?"

"We're here to install your new servers."

James looked around to see if they were possibly talking to someone else. "That contract was only signed on Friday... afternoon."

The man looked at a clipboard. "We have an order here that says these servers are to be installed and set up immediately, correctly, and are to be working perfectly by the end of the day... or else."

The man turned the clipboard around so James could see the work order. It included a handwritten note that did in fact end with the words "or else." It wasn't Gabe's handwriting, but there was definite emphasis behind the words.

"Okay. Follow me, then." James led them down to the server room. He looked around at the missing floor tiles and exposed cables and felt like he had unexpected house guests and hadn't picked up first. He showed them to the space once occupied by Mister McFeely. "There we go."

Martin, who was studying networking, showed up as the guys were breaking into the boxes. He picked up one of the user manuals that had come with boxes and flipped it open to the page listing all the vitals. He made a rather inappropriate noise.

"Boss, if you don't want your boyfriend, I'll take him."

"You're straight."

Martin held up the page that listed the RAM, storage, and processing power of the box. "For this, I'd go there."

James noticed the TechPrim guys had their eyes focused

firmly on their work. He took the manual away from Martin. "Go get the cabling binder so we're not trying to update it in a month."

James pulled out his phone to send a quick text. Normally he got irritated when people tried to interfere with his job, but he was looking at a new TPARC 12 core 3.6Ghz N6-32x server with 32 terabytes of memory and a service agreement that could make a grown man weep. That bought a lot of forgiveness.

Thank you.

A minute later James got a text that was a colon, a dash, and a star. He stared at it until Martin got back.

"Martin, what's this emoticon?" He hoped it wasn't rude, but he didn't think Gabe would send anything like that.

Martin laughed. "It's a kiss."

James looked at it again and tilted his head. "Oh! Okay."

He hit reply and texted back a kiss in return.

7

Gabe sighed as his body cooled against his new sheets, and his head settled onto James' naked thigh. It had been an exhausting bitch of a week. He hadn't had more than four hours' sleep on any given night. He hadn't even been able to find time to call James more than once. For a week almost, their entire relationship had been conducted via text messages. That might work for young people, but by Friday evening, Gabe desperately wanted to actually hear James' voice—in person if at all possible.

James' fingers stroked through Gabe's hair.

It hadn't been their most energetic tumble, but it had been soft and sweet and had drained the last of Gabe's energy from his body. He yawned. "Sorry."

"It's okay. You look exhausted."

"I feel exhausted."

"You should sleep, then."

"My phone is probably going to ring any second." Gabe had started to hear it ring in his sleep, only to wake up and find it silent.

"I'm sorry."

Gabe closed his eyes as James' fingers slipped through his curls, and with a soft breath, he slept.

When he opened his eyes, his head was on a pillow, a blanket had been pulled over his body, and his fingers were interlaced with James'. He wondered if he'd been chewing on them in his sleep or if James had noticed that a few of them were going raw after the last week.

He didn't ask because James was fast asleep and the room was dark. Gabe must have already been asleep when James pulled up the blankets and turned off the lights. For once his phone didn't seem to be ringing. He closed his eyes and drifted back to sleep.

When Gabe's phone did finally ring, it was early, but at least the sun was up. He fumbled for it but didn't recognize the number coming in. He sent it to voice mail, hoping it wouldn't wake James, but it was too late, and James was already sitting up.

"Hey, how'd you sleep?" James' voice sounded gravelly, and he cleared his throat.

"Good. Surprised my phone didn't ring. You should go back to sleep, though. Get a few more hours."

James stretched. "I'm awake. I'm usually up at this hour."

Gabe pulled him close so James was cuddled up against his body. "Have you got plans for the weekend?" Gabe might have been told, but his mind was so muddled from too much work and not enough sleep that he could have easily forgotten.

"Just regular stuff. Laundry, shopping. Might have dinner with my parents on Sunday. Dylan's got some big tests and essays coming up, so he's going to have his head in his books all weekend. In theory at any rate."

"What you're saying is you don't have to dash away at any point this morning?" That was exactly what Gabe wanted to hear.

"Not unless our new server catches fire. Thank you for that, by the way."

"My pleasure. This job has got to have a couple of perks."

"A couple?"

He caught James' lips in a kiss. "Well, it does have a bad habit of cutting into my boyfriend time, and there aren't many perks that can make up for that." James didn't reply, just kissed him back.

The sun was a good deal higher in the sky, and Gabe had let two more calls go to messages by the time they rolled out of bed and into the shower. He wasn't up for another round as he stood under the spray, James' body spooned against his, but he wished he was. From the other room, he could just make out the sound of his phone. He was tempted to go get it just so he could drown the thing.

He told himself it was the job. It was the job he loved. It made him a fortune. He got to work with his best friends. He got to see the world and put in motion ideas that would change that world. It was also the job every single boyfriend had dumped him over. They usually had other excuses; they met someone else, they were moving, they felt there were compatibility issues, but at the end of the day, it was the job. Always the job.

He gave James an extra squeeze and tried to shake the ghost of relationships past from his head. James felt too nice in his arms to be thinking about all of that.

James twisted around in his arms and laid his head against Gabe's shoulder. "We should get out soon. We'll get all wrinkly."

"Yeah," Gabe agreed but made no move to leave. In the distance a phone rang. He squeezed his eyes shut and tightened his arms around James.

James squeezed him back. "I'm sure you'll get everything done that you need to."

"I'm sure I will too. Doesn't mean camping out at a high-altitude lake with no cell coverage doesn't sound really appealing right now."

James rubbed his back. "I'm sorry."

"No, it's my own damn fault. I just need to take a deep breath, keep focused, and push through. Eye on the prize and all that shit."

The phone stopped ringing. James gave him another hug, then pulled away. "We should get breakfast in you." James smiled, but it seemed hesitant.

Shit, Gabe thought. He should have learned by now to be careful talking about work in front of any boyfriend. He pulled James back in close for a deep, hard kiss until he felt James begin to melt in his arms. Maybe he was up for another round after all.

GABE LICKED the last of the syrup from the french toast off his lips. It was his favorite "looks fancy but is actually really easy" breakfast recipe. James tipped his head back, draining his coffee, showing off his neck. Gabe licked his lips again. He was well past the age where he could go three rounds in one morning, but that didn't mean he couldn't appreciate what was in front of him. And he did love James in that blue robe. That shimmer of silk looked good against his skin, and it showed off his body in the most appealing manner.

That thought caused a mental note to pop up in his head. He drained his own coffee and went rummaging through the "random stuff" drawer in his kitchen.

"What are you looking for?"

"This." Gabe pulled out a long tape measure as well as a small notebook and pencil.

"Okay? And what are you planning on measuring with that?"

"You. For a tux."

"Um…."

"I did say I'd arrange one. I mean, I could call my tailor and have him swing by with some fabric swatches and—"

"I'm sure it'll be fine, whatever you pick," James said quickly.

"Great, stand up."

Gabe's tailor would throw a fit, sewing up something for someone he'd never met, and probably double the price in punishment, but Gabe couldn't tell James he was having one custom made. It was a balancing act. The boyfriend of the CFO could not show up to prom in a rented tux, but there was no way James' pride would handle a custom-made one purchased for one event. Gabe hoped "what James didn't know couldn't hurt him" would stand up on this occasion.

He'd been fitted for enough suits that he knew exactly how to take every measurement, including ones most people don't think of, like waist-to-hips, and circumferences of wrists and ankles.

"Is that really necessary?" James asked as Gabe measured his foot.

"Want to make sure you don't get shoes that are too tight. Nothing worse than dress shoes that don't fit correctly." He kissed the inside of James' ankle.

"Now, I'm pretty sure that's not what usually happens when people get fitted for clothes."

Gabe put a kiss on the side of his knee before standing up.

"Any other bit of me you need to measure?" James asked, a quirk in his lips.

"Nope. And I'll pick out something nice for you. Don't worry."

"I'm not. Besides, you're the one who's going to have to be seen in public with me."

Gabe pulled James into his arms. "You say that like it's a bad thing." James shrugged, and in the other room, Gabe's phone rang. He didn't let go of James, though. "I was thinking, maybe the next time you come over, you can bring a spare shirt and leave it here."

"Why?" James looked genuinely confused.

"Well, I keep sending you home in the same clothes I pick you up in. I thought you might want to leave a few things here —" James eyes went wide. Gabe recognized the start of one of James' smaller panic episodes. "If you want," he added quickly, hoping to calm James down. "I just thought it would be more convenient for you."

"Yeah. Sure," James answered, even as he started to pull away. "It's a good idea."

Gabe quietly kicked himself but was thankful he hadn't jumped right into the "Why don't you quit your crappy job and move in with me" pitch. Gabe's phone rang again. He ignored it but also used it to change the topic.

"I was also thinking if you don't have to run home right away, I can ignore my phone for a bit more. We could take a drive up to Half Moon Bay. Dip our toes in the ocean. Take a hike. Get lunch?"

"Can you afford to do that?"

The phone had stopped ringing. Gabe thought, *Can I afford not to?*

JAMES STRIPPED off his shoes and socks as soon as he came through his door. As much as he tried to brush the beach sand off his feet, some always managed to stick.

"Hey, Dad. We're in here," Dylan called out from the kitchen. James wondered who the "we" was.

In the kitchen a slightly frumpy brunette with glasses perched on the end of her nose sat across from Dylan. James was ashamed to admit that his first thought was that she didn't seem like Dylan's usual type, until he noticed the chemistry books and stacks of notes.

"Dad, you remember Melinda."

"Of course. Hi." James knew he'd always now remember Melinda as the girl Dylan got into a fight for.

"Hello, Mr. Maron." Melinda gave a painfully shy little smile.

"How's this all going?" James waved his hand over the pile of books.

Dylan said, "Miserable," at the same moment Melinda said, "Fine."

"Do you have any tricks for memorizing lists of ions?" Dylan asked.

"My strongest memory of high school chemistry was the day I took notes in blue crayon because I couldn't find a regular pen anywhere in my bag."

Dylan closed his eyes. "Okay."

James wished he could help, but he wasn't kidding when he said that most of high school was little more than an exhausted blur. "Sorry. I'm sure you'll do fine."

"Thanks. Oh, and Grandma called. She wants us over for dinner tomorrow."

"Do I need to call her back?"

"Nah."

"Okay. I'm going to do laundry. You two keep at it."

James wandered into his bedroom but bypassed the basket of dirty laundry that sat in the corner. He sat on his bed and listened to it squeak under him. He'd never really noticed it squeaking before. He stared at the laundry basket with a blue button-down shirt sitting on top. It was a work shirt but not one of his main ones. He figured it would be okay to leave it at Gabe's place. When Gabe had mentioned it, he'd felt panic settle into his chest, though he couldn't work out why. There was nothing wrong with Gabe suggesting he leave a spare shirt. It was perfectly practical, and he liked practical. It meant Gabe was serious. He liked serious. Gabe just wanted him to be comfortable. James ran his hands over his face. It was too much to think about. It was probably best to just keep taking the whole thing one step at a time, instead of letting his brain rush ahead. Gabe almost certainly had his brain fully on the Russians and Solar Flare, and he didn't need James complicating things by reading too much into a practical little suggestion.

He sighed, picked up the laundry basket, and decided to get to work.

8

Gabe unzipped the heavy suit bag that had been left for him at his building's concierge desk. His tailor had thrown a very quiet and dignified fit when he'd handed over James' measurements and informed him that he wasn't actually going to get to adjust it with James in it.

To appease him Gabe had taken a reasonable amount of time out of a particularly backed-up schedule to pick out styles, fabrics, and accessories. He'd decided on a slightly unusual silk/wool blend that looked like it would drape nicely on James' frame, the silk giving depth to the black wool.

He pulled the jacket from the bag and held it up. He couldn't wait to see James in it. He couldn't wait for other people to see James in it. The truth was, he'd never taken anyone to the TechPrim birthday party. He'd either been single or he'd been seeing flaky party boys that his employees did not need to be exposed to. James, however, was someone he wanted to introduce to his VPs and department heads. He wanted pictures of the two of them dressed up and looking happy together to appear in the weekend gossip roundup, instead of secret long-lens shots.

Gabe took out his phone.

How is your day going? Home yet?

He hit send and opened one of the boxes that came with the suit bag. The fine linen shirt he had ordered was gleaming white and carefully starched. He'd thought about getting a colored one, but that was something that really needed to be tried on first.

Gabe's phone bleeped.

Looking at rental tuxes with Dylan. He's got prom in a couple of weeks. Feeling old.

Gabe grinned.

You are not old. Tell him to look for something in an English-style jacket. The last thing he needs is more padding on his shoulders. Also mid-sized lapels.

Gabe had fairly broad shoulders himself and the continental-style jackets made him look like a linebacker. On Dylan they'd make him look like a brick wall, and Gabe had the feeling Catherine wouldn't be into that.

I think we'll be taking what we can get.

Gabe sighed and ran his hand against the elegant linen of the shirt James would be wearing in just a few days.

Then recommend he stick with a classic look. Remind him his kids will be seeing the photos in twenty years and he doesn't want to be too embarrassed by them.

:-) I'll be sure to pass that along.

THE LITTLE CLOCK on the corner of James' computer screen crawled toward the weekend. He drummed his fingers along the top of his mouse, staring at the numbers. While he couldn't claim to love his job, he was usually pretty Zen about Friday afternoons. But then he usually didn't have plans for the weekend that counted for much.

He was supposed to be answering some e-mails, but the people who wanted replies had already left for the weekend, so there was not exactly a rush. He could put them off until Monday morning if he had to. He drummed his fingers some more and stared up at the pencils jammed into the ceiling over his head.

After a considerable amount of teasing on Dylan's part last night, James looked up pictures online from previous TechPrim proms. There were a bunch buried in the company website and others on various gossip blogs. There were lots of pictures of Gabe, Nate, and Frank in tuxedos looking quite good. Almost all of them had Gabe standing in between the other two. There were plenty of Nate and Margaret as well, plus Frank with a woman he didn't recognize. It took an hour of procrastinating and digging deep into the net for James to realize that there were no pictures of Gabe with anyone he didn't work with. Even reading through the three sentence write-ups, none even hinted about Gabe in a relationship.

That realization sent some odd half-formed emotions swirling. More digging through old gossip pages had Gabe on the sidelines of Frank's divorce and apparently a third marriage. Any reported romances were either with Tamyra or some other random woman he happened to be standing next to when whatever picture was taken.

And now James was going to the TechPrim prom. A courier had dropped off a clothing bag for him that afternoon. He'd only peeked into the bag and run his fingers along the deep black fabric. It felt amazingly soft but strong and miles away from the tuxes he and Dylan had been looking over the day before. Considering the number of measurements Gabe took and quality of the material he knew it wasn't a rental of any kind. Gabe had gone to a tailor with those measurements, picked out fabrics, styles, accessories.

The part of him that had nearly cried when filling out food-stamp forms fifteen years earlier, was positively screaming at the thought of a tux made just for him for this night. Another part of him wished that Gabe wasn't the CFO so he could have just rented a tux like a normal person, had a fun night, and not thought about the ramifications that he was the first man Gabe had ever been public with. And yet a third part of his mind was screaming at the other two to just shut the fuck up because he was getting sex and nice gifts, and was generally happy, and that was not a bad thing. All in all the inside of his head was getting noisy.

James never kept a drop of alcohol in his apartment, but Mrs. Avila liked to put enough rum in her coffee that it was more rum than coffee, and she was always more than willing to share. She also wouldn't hesitate to smack down his pride when it started getting in the way.

He watched the clock flip to five thirty. He shut down his computer as quickly as possible. He really needed some coffee.

GABE GAVE a spin in his stocking feet, letting himself whirl around his office bathroom. He'd gotten in early so he could do some quick weekend work before the party. Crews had already been in the lobby setting up tables, stringing lights, and setting up a stage. The prom always looked good and went off well, but he wanted this year to be perfect. Truthfully, while he always looked forward to the annual party, he hadn't been this excited about it in years. If there was one night to show off TechPrim, it was prom night.

He ran some gel through his hair, still damp from a quick shower. His phone pinged at him, telling him he had a text. He peered at it surprised to see his sister's name. She wasn't much for texting.

Mom is going to call you in a minute. Be warned.

A string of curses in multiple languages filled his mind.

Why?

Not sure. Just know she's on the phone with Auntie Loreen and heard Cousin Felipe's name, then yours.

"Crap," Gabe muttered. Before he could reply to that text, his phone began to ring with his mother's picture up on the screen.

"Dylan!" James called out, finally hitting the limit of his frustrations.

"What?" Dylan shouted back before entering the bedroom.

"By some odd chance, do you know how to tie a bow tie?" He held out the offending strip of black silk. "I've looked at these instructions about fifty times."

"Give them here." James handed over the tie and an instruction guide he'd printed out at work the day before. Dylan read them over a few times before placing the tie around James' neck. "Who'd've thought I'd be helping you get ready for prom?" James rolled his eyes but didn't comment. Dylan pulled his hands away, then frowned. "Let me try that again." James stood there, head back, while Dylan made a half-dozen attempts.

"Maybe you can forget about the tie?" Dylan asked, admitting defeat himself.

"It's a black-tie event. Tie is sort of in the description."

"You can do that whole, hang it around your neck like you're just too cool to bother tying it. Sort of a Daniel Craig-Bond-look."

"No one is ever going to believe I'm too cool for anything."

Dylan draped the tie around James' neck anyway. "Get Gabe to do it for you. Let's get the rest of you done up." He grabbed the cufflinks that were lying on the bed. They were heavy silver with dark mother-of-pearl inlay and had been tucked in with the shirt. Dylan slid them into place before helping James with the jacket and smoothing down the lapels.

"Look at you, Dad."

James looked at himself in the little mirror that hung inside his wardrobe door. He truly didn't recognize himself. He pulled his shoulders back. He seemed taller, slim without being skinny, and there were no strange wrinkles. There was nothing worn, faded, or patched. He couldn't even see a loose thread. He was almost afraid to move. The jacket sat perfectly on his shoulders like a work of art, a study of clean lines in black.

Dylan shifted his hair around so it looked halfway good. He gave each sleeve a quick tug. The cufflinks glinted in the light of the single bulb. He wiggled his toes in his shoes and wondered what the socks that he had found tucked into them were made of. They felt awfully nice.

He turned to face Dylan. "How do I look?"

Dylan looked him over, his head tilted to one side. "You look like a grown-up." James sighed at the glib response. "No, I mean it. You look like you are about to go off to a very swank party on the arm of a captain of industry, and you look like that's exactly where you're supposed to be going." Dylan smiled, looking positively proud. "You don't look like you're going to prom."

James looked at himself in the mirror again and brushed his hand down the lapels. His phone rang, and he quickly grabbed it. He was finally getting to the point where he recognized the ringtone.

"Hello?"

"Hi. It's me." Gabe sounded breathless. "Did the tux get there? Did it fit okay?"

"It fits great. What's up?"

"I'm really sorry." James' stomach dropped as Gabe rattled off the words. "I got a hell of a mess dropped in my lap, so I'm not going to be able to drive up there to get you if I want to actually be able to spend any time at the party."

"Oh, okay. I can get down there—" He'd have to try out the map function on his phone to actually find the TechPrim offices.

"Don't be silly. I talked Jared into heading up there. He should be there any moment now."

"Oh, um… okay, then."

"I swear I was going to call you about an hour ago, but this is the first moment I've had—"

"It's okay, really." Gabe sounded frantic, something James had never heard from him before.

"It *really* isn't, and if I could disown my entire family at this point and—" Gabe cut himself off and took a deep breath. "Everything is okay with the tux?"

James glanced at himself in the mirror again. "Yeah. The tux is good. Still working on the tie a bit."

Gabe laughed. "Don't worry about that. I still need to get Margaret or Tamyra to do mine. If they're not around, I just dangle it around my neck and try to look cool."

"For some reason I think you could pull off that look better than I could."

"Don't underestimate your coolness." There were voices in the background of the call. "Okay, I've got to go. I'll see you soon?"

"See you soon. Bye." Dylan looked at him questioningly. "Something big popped up, so Jared's going to be picking me up instead of Gabe himself." Dylan pinched his lips, giving a disapproving look he must have picked up from his grandmother. "He's got a lot of important work. It's amazing he gets any time."

Dylan straightened James' collar. "You are important too. And I think he's just trying to avoid me taking photos."

"Quite possibly. But I'm sure there are going to be plenty of photos on the net by tomorrow morning."

Dylan was still scowling when there was a knock on the door. "I'll get it." Dylan rushed to the front door while James tried to work out how to stick his wallet and keys into a pocket without it causing strange lumps. In the end he just yanked out his driver's license, cash card, and house key and slipped it into his phone case. The ultra slim P22X was nearly invisible as he slipped it into his jacket.

Jared stood in the living room in his own flawless tux. "Hey, James. Looking good."

"Thanks. You look nice too. And thank you for coming up here. I'm sure boyfriend collection isn't exactly in your contract."

Jared grinned. "Don't worry about it. I owe Gabe a couple. The boss was pretty damned pissed that he couldn't come up himself, but some big family-related ball of shit hit some fan somewhere. Do you need help with that?" Jared pointed to the tie James was still holding.

"I am ashamed to say, but yes."

Jared took the tie from his hand. "My first unit commander taught me how to do this." James barely had time to tilt his head back before the tie was secure around his neck.

He gave a little cough. "Here's to military efficiency."

"One sec." Dylan pulled out his own phone. "Dad, smile." James smiled, and the phone beeped. "Perfect. Now go, have a good night. And yes, I'll be good, and I won't have girls over." Dylan made little shooing motions.

"Okay, I'll go. Be good," James added, despite Dylan's assurances.

The car was parked in front of the building. James let himself into the front seat once it was unlocked. It felt too weird riding in the back with Gabe not there.

"So. Army?" James asked. He and Jared had never actually had a conversation.

"260th Quartermaster Battalion. Our job was mainly to get fuel where it needed to go. Areas where there aren't exactly gas stations on every corner."

"I can see how that would be vitally important."

"I'll take this gig over that any day. For as bad as Bay Area traffic gets, there's *usually* no one shooting at you."

GABE HUNG up the phone for hopefully the final time just as Tamyra slid into his office. He took half a second to look her over. She might be a lesbian and he might be gay, but he was gay, not dead. Her hair tumbled down her back in a mass of carefully styled curls. Her floor-length, black, backless dress hugged her body, drawing the eye to all the right places, and she moved in it like a runway model. She looked ready to walk down the red carpet at the Oscars, as elegant as the biggest stars.

"Come on, Boss. The GPS on the car says your boyfriend is about ten minutes away."

"Oh, good." Gabe picked up his tie from the desk and held it out. "Do you mind?"

She took it from his hand. "One of these days, you're going to have to learn to do this yourself."

"Why? I've got you."

"Yes, yes, you do." Tamyra gave the tie a yank, and Gabe choked a little.

"Hey, since we're on the topic, I have something for you. A sort of 'Thank you for putting up with my shit for so long' gift." He pulled a small box out of his desk drawer and handed it to her.

"You didn't have to."

"No, really, I sort of did."

She flipped the lid open, and her jaw dropped. Gabe decided it was worth the cost for that expression alone. He'd found three perfect teardrop rubies that were just walking the line between large and tacky. He'd had the largest one set as a necklace and the two smaller ones as earrings. He was particularly happy with the settings. They were in the early art-deco style that appeared in a lot of Tamyra's design and jewelry choices.

"Do you like them?"

Tamyra just nodded.

"Oh, good. I wasn't sure."

She nodded again, then her brows came together in thought. "Who helped you pick this out?"

"You don't think I'm capable of buying jewelry for a woman without help?" She leveled a disbelieving look at him. "I asked Dylan for some advice."

"Smart move."

"Here." Gabe picked up the necklace, and Tamyra turned around. He fiddled with the tiny clasp for a moment before getting it around her long neck.

She turned back around. He seemed to have gauged the length right, as it hung neatly above her cleavage. She looked down at it. "Thank you. It's beautiful."

He gave her a peck on the cheek. "Only the best for the world's greatest PA."

She picked up the earrings and traded them for the gold ones she'd been wearing. "Sara and Christine are going to be jealous."

"That's Frank and Nate's problem. And neither of them have put in a decade yet."

"They're getting close."

"Again, Frank and Nate's problem."

Tamyra did a quick spin around. "How do I look?"

"Like a million bucks."

"That's chump change around here."

"Okay, a billion."

"That's better." She grabbed his coat from the back of his chair and held it up. "Come on now. We don't want to keep James waiting."

"No, we really don't."

Gabe tried to calm himself down before hitting the main party. When they had built the new TechPrim campus, he had the huge lobby designed so it could hold everyone plus partners for the birthday party. Tables brimming with food and drink lined the vast multilevel space, along with some chairs, a dance floor, and a small stage for the band. Large screens were mounted all over the lobby, showing parties in progress at other TechPrim outposts across the globe.

The space had already begun to fill with smiling people in gowns and tuxes. It gave the room sparkle and elegance but without the slick air of snobbery that permeated the majority of formal events Gabe was forced to attend. As he headed toward the main doors, he smiled, nodded to employees as they passed, and shook hands with some of the VPs and higher-level executives. Then he saw James step through the main doors. James instantly looked up at the lobby's cathedral-like arches of formed golden wood and a ceiling of glass. Gabe had wanted that reaction, for people to look up like they were stepping into a great church, but instead of seeing saints or arches of stone, he wanted them to see the vastness of the sky.

James lowered his head as Gabe walked up to him. "You like the view?" The sky was a gradient of blues flowing into lavender from the last hints of the setting sun.

"I like it."

Gabe gave him a peck on the cheek. "I'm so sorry I couldn't come up to get you. Believe me, I wish I could have. There was this stuff with my cousins and—"

James took his hand. "It's okay. I got here, and you're here. That's what matters."

Gabe gave him another quick kiss, unbelievably grateful for James' understanding nature, and looked him over. He made a mental note to send a thank-you note to his tailor. James looked just stunning. The tuxedo highlighted his slim figure, making him look taller, and Gabe was willing to bet his backside would look great. The urge to take James straight up to his office, lock the door, and totally ruin the couch was hard to fight.

"You look great, by the way."

James looked down at himself. "You picked it out. You look very nice too."

"Thanks. Come on." Gabe held out his elbow, and James took it. The band had finished setting up. The canned music faded down before the lead singer started on some Rat Pack standards. James kept craning his neck to look around the vast lobby.

"So, this is TechPrim?"

"I like to think of TechPrim more as a nebulous concept brought to form by the hard work of loyal and dedicated employees." James looked at him smiling but with his lips pinched tight like he was trying not to laugh. Something that pretentious-sounding deserved a laugh, and Gabe tried not to laugh at himself. "Yeah, this is TechPrim. When we were just laying out the groundwork for all this, one of our main competitors was also working on their campus. We got ahold of the blueprints for their lobby."

"And you went and built a bigger one."

"We were going to do it anyway. Of course that company crashed and burned about three years ago, got split up and sold off bit by bit. We scraped up their entire design department and use their campus as overflow space."

"I'm incredibly ashamed to admit it, but I might be just a little bit turned on."

Gabe grinned. "TechPrim treats their employees very well on the benefits and working-conditions front. I figure that's got to get us a bit of good Karma every time we envelop a competitor." He grabbed a couple of glasses of champagne off a table. It wasn't Veuve Clicquot, the company wasn't doing that well, but it was still of a decent quality. He handed one to James. "You do look very nice tonight."

James tried to pull down his cuffs a little. "Thank you."

Gabe watched a bubble loose itself from the inside of his glass and race to the top. "What shall we drink to?"

James stared at his own glass. "To good Karma."

Gabe raised his and clinked the two together. "To good Karma."

———

JAMES SIPPED his champagne and did his best not to just openly ogle Gabe. He always dressed well in custom-tailored suits, but there was something about the tux Gabe had chosen for that night. He wondered if it was the Bond effect, if the fact that it was a tux suddenly gave Gabe an extra level of cool with a hint of danger.

Maybe it was the way Gabe strolled through the crowd. He didn't even have to say "excuse me." He was the boss, and they parted before him. Gabe gave him a flirtatious little smile at the same time James saw a couple whispering over Gabe's shoulder. They could have been talking about anyone, but eyes flicked his way.

James shifted, suddenly feeling uncomfortable. He wasn't used to spending time in anyone's, even secondhand, spotlight. Gabe looked over his shoulder at the couple that had been talking, then took his hand. "Hey, I sign the paychecks. If anyone has a problem, they are going to keep very quiet about it."

The couple who had been whispering looked away and joined some other couple in conversation. James took another sip of his champagne, just as Frank, Nate, and Margaret approached. A tall woman in a slinky red dress, whom James didn't recognize, came with them. Margaret was particularly elegant in a sleeveless dress of midnight blue that swept along the ground.

"James." She gave him a hug. "Don't you look nice tonight."

"Thank you. You look good too."

"Oh, I don't think you've met Frank's wife, Cassandra."

There were quick handshakes. "Pleasure."

James had hoped that Margaret would be around. He had gotten along well with her and they had the comfortable common ground of trying to raise teenagers.

She leaned toward him. "Overwhelmed yet?"

James sipped his champagne, trying to look cool. "Nice little shindig." He got a few chuckles off that one.

"Have you eaten?" Gabe asked.

"Not really." James had spent the afternoon trying to tie his tie. Food had slipped his mind.

"Let's grab something before the interns hoover it all up." There were nods and smiles as everyone separated to mingle. The tables set around the edge of the party groaned with what looked like enough food to feed a small army. James looked over his shoulder at the still-growing crowd. It looked like small army was exactly how many people it needed to feed. He eyed two punch bowls full of chicken wings. In one they were swimming in sauce; the others were fried.

"We used to go with elaborate themes for the food each year, but a few years back we finally realized that after a couple drinks, most people just wanted to scarf chicken wings and crab puffs."

James grabbed one of the fried wings, well aware of the pristine white shirt he was wearing. "I think I can appreciate that."

Gabe gave him a peck on the cheek and grabbed a fried one himself. James felt himself flush. Gabe had kissed him on the cheek plenty of times, but he was acutely aware of the steadily growing crowd behind him.

"What's wrong?"

"Nothing." James shoved the bite of chicken in his mouth as Gabe squinted at him. It was easily the best chicken he'd ever tasted. He wondered just how much effort some fancy chef must have put into two bites of chicken. He washed it down with a sip of champagne.

"I have to do at least one spin around the room, saying hi to everyone. That all right?"

"Your party." James was eying up more chicken wings.

"Great." Gabe took his arm again, and they waded into the crowd. James was startled. He glanced over his shoulder at the wings. He had thought Gabe would leave him by the wall while he went and talked to people. Instead he found himself introduced to VPs, department heads, and team leads. He smiled, shook hands. It felt a bit like that first proper date at the country club again, except these people actually tried to make small talk with him, and didn't give him so much as a sideways glance when Gabe introduced him as his boyfriend.

As each new person smiled at them with unfailing politeness and deference, it began to sink in that Gabe wasn't just the boss. He was a prince, and TechPrim his vast, imperial kingdom. Yet he didn't lord himself over anyone. He had equal time for a silver-haired VP or a pimply faced junior engineer, but when he moved, the crowd parted before him, stopping just short of a bow and curtsy. He caught a glimpse of Frank or Nate a few times, and while everyone was polite to them as well, neither radiated the raw charisma that Gabe embodied.

And James was locked to the hip of that charisma, with Gabe often swinging an arm low around his waist, even as he had light conversations about R&D ideas and strange market trends. He couldn't figure out if it was the attention or the champagne that was making him a little dizzy. He was intensely relieved when he saw Tamyra step out of the crowd, looking stunning.

"Hey, Boss. James. You look good."

"So do you." James tried not to stare, but it was hard to ignore real beauty, even if there was no physical attraction.

"Boss, you and the guys need to get ready to go on stage. And I'm going to borrow James for a minute."

James looked around, wondering what Tamyra could want him for. "Um…. Okay?"

Tamyra snaked her arm around James and led him away before Gabe had a chance to comment. She dragged him over to one of the smaller food tables.

"What do you need?" James asked.

"Nothing. But you looked like you were about to pass out if you had to shake hands with one more department head. Here." She handed him a minipirozhki. "Eat something."

"Thank you." James was aware he'd had more champagne than solid food.

"Don't worry about it. He's gotten used to this place just getting bigger every day. I don't think he gets what it's like to jump into the deep end."

"It's… um… a little intense."

"Somewhere in his head, this place is still a start-up with ten employees, and this is all just a stack of pizzas and a case of beer. As a result it is perfectly reasonable to say hi to everyone and know all their names."

James looked over his shoulder at the crowd that still seemed to be growing. "I don't think I could tell you the name of a single person I just met."

"You better believe they all know your name. I've worked for Gabe for ten years now, and while he's never been in the closet, he's never exactly been public with anyone."

"I kinda got that impression." James looked over the crowd again and noticed a small group of quite attractive young men looking his way. He didn't think Gabe would be the type to date an employee, but he certainly had options if he wanted. "Not sure why me but—" James still didn't know what had possibly made him stand out to Gabe.

"Seriously?" Tamyra stared at him incredulously. "Gabe has…. Okay, not bad taste in men, usually, but lazy taste in men. Either pretty and dumb or guys that already have one foot out the door and one eye on his bank account. I don't think he even particularly liked half of his boyfriends. You, he likes. A lot. You're a good person. You confuse the crap out of him some days because you don't react the way his one-week wonders reacted, but frankly that's good for him. He needs to take time out for something other than the company. He needs to put some effort into someone other than the company."

"I wouldn't want him to—"

Tamyra shoved another pirozhki into his mouth, cutting off any objections.

The music died down, and everyone turned toward the stage.

Gabe, Frank, Nate, and Margaret stepped up onto the stage to loud applause. Gabe waved his hands, and the crowd settled down. He stepped up to the microphone, grinning broadly.

"Thank you all. Is everyone having a good time this evening?"

There were some cheers from the crowd followed by delayed applause from the screens.

"Good, good. I'm going to try to keep this quick, but for those of you who haven't noticed, in the last year we've added many new faces to the TechPrim family, all over the world, and

I'd just like to say welcome to all of you having your first birthday celebration here with us tonight."

There was another round of applause followed by a good deal more from the more far-flung outposts of the TechPrim empire.

"I know one of the sayings punted around these days is 'corporations are people.' Now as far as I'm concerned, that's a whole load of horse droppings, but corporations are made of people, and in the case of TechPrim, good, honest, loyal people with whom it is an honor and a privilege to work."

The crowd applauded again, and Gabe plucked the microphone from the stand.

"Now I've told this story before, but we have a lot of new people this year, so bear with me if you've heard this one. Many years ago, two nerds and their poor put-upon dorm-mate decided to start a company. Due to a typo on the trademark registration application that was being filled out at three in the morning, the company was called TechPrim. Our first office was smaller than this stage and was in a basement. It had an air conditioner that leaked, only two phone lines, and the power went out at least once a week. Our reception area consisted of a sofa, and our dear Margaret would show up once a week and pretend to be our receptionist."

A chuckle went around the crowd.

"We couldn't even afford a company sign. I had a cousin carve 'TechPrim' into an aluminum sheet during shop class. No one thought we'd make it six months. A year wasn't even thinkable. And we weren't the only start-up in our building. In the eight floors above us, there were seventeen other start-ups. Of course they had real reception areas, noninstant coffee, and lights that worked. They'd all taken venture capital money, or huge loans against products that didn't yet exist. One day when TechPrim was just coming up on its first full year in business, we were all there late, and we saw some of our business neighbors stumble by in fancy clothes with a bottle of expensive champagne, celebrating six months of business on the company budget. The next week was TechPrim's birthday, and we decided we were going to party as well. Frank, Nate, and I rented tuxedos. Margaret dragged out her old prom dress, and we went down to Denny's and split a chocolate sundae four ways out of petty cash."

The smile on Gabe's face had slipped into one that usually came out only in more private places. James recognized it as the one Gabe had when he was thinking fondly about someone.

"As I said, that was a long time ago. Of those seventeen companies we shared that building with, eleven were out of business within two years. Four of the remaining six were bought up, and two merged and were later bought up as well. And as of January, TechPrim now owns the companies that bought those final six."

Another cheer went up from the crowd.

"We survived. And then we thrived. We expanded. Commercial offices on six continents and the Antarctic research stations all use our products. Even in these difficult times, TechPrim is a company that stands strong in the face of all opposition. And while TechPrim may have started with the four of us here, it could never have thrived the way it has if it was just us. Our success as a company can be linked directly to the hard work of each and every one of you. Look around—you are TechPrim. This is the house that you built and will continue to build. And you should be proud of that. There are some big things on the horizon in the coming years, but for tonight, please, relax and enjoy this evening. We've come a long way from a single chocolate sundae and have so much further yet to go, and I just know that journey is going to be remarkable, and I'm glad we're taking it together. So thank you, thank you all."

Frank and Nate both leaned in and said some brief thanks into the microphone, but the real applause was for Gabe, and James found himself applauding as well.

Tamyra leaned in close. "Yes, he's been asked to run for office."

Gabe strode off the stage and into the crowd of his employees/subjects. That speech had done nothing if not reinforce the image of Gabe as some beloved crown prince within these walls.

He shook hands with several people as the band started back up. James looked up at one of the screens where the celebrants at another party were dancing to something probably a lot louder, judging by the attempts at head banging by guys far too old for it.

The crowd split up into those headed for more drinks or food and a few brave couples who were taking to the dance floor with slow swaying. Gabe slid out from the crowd.

"How are you doing? Enjoying yourself?" he asked with a smile.

"I'm fine," James answered automatically, despite still feeling overwhelmed. "Though I feel like I should be whistling 'Hail to the Chief' or something."

"I would make a terrible politician. I'm far too accustomed to getting my own way."

"I'd vote for you."

"That's good to know." Gabe held out his hand. "Can I talk you into a dance?"

"I really don't—"

"Yes, you do, and you dance fine." Gabe took his hand and guided him to the dance floor. There were already two women in evening gowns dancing together, so he couldn't exactly object on that front. Gabe gave him puppy dog eyes. "Please?"

James felt his heart begin to race and his throat tighten with nerves. "Okay."

Another slow song started, and Gabe pulled him close, helping James find the rhythm.

He felt strange dancing; it was even odder to be dancing with someone, and to be doing that in front of a large audience was flat-out weird. But Gabe led with confidence, easing his nerves, as they swayed on the dance floor among other couples. James let the music flow over him and melted into the warmth of Gabe's body. He felt light. It could be the champagne, but his limbs felt loose, and his mind didn't want to settle on any one thought until it was finally resting in a sort of white-noise haze. The music finished, and he looked up into Gabe's eyes. Gabe looked back, and his breath caught in his throat. Gabe brushed a bit of hair away from his face. Another song started, but they didn't move.

"Would you mind terribly if we said our good nights?" Gabe asked softly, sounding tired.

"No."

Gabe kissed him on the cheek. "Meet you by the door? I'll be right there."

"Sure."

Gabe moved through the dancers toward Nate and Frank, who were swaying with their wives. James strolled through the party, occasionally looking up at the screens still broadcasting. One showed someone slumped in a chair, drooling, in an empty office. On other screens the parties were still going strong.

Gabe met him by the wide glass doors. "I ordered us a car."

"Okay."

Gabe gave him a small, soft kiss. "I'm really glad you came tonight."

"I'm glad I came too."

The doors slid open. A Town Car was waiting at the curb. They didn't talk as they made the short trip to Gabe's building. They just held hands and watched the lights go past outside.

They didn't even talk as the elevator took them swiftly and smoothly up to Gabe's place. The lights automatically came on as they stepped out of the elevator, neither too fast nor too bright; a soft fade-up to a warm glow.

Gabe stepped close and pulled on James' bow tie until it came loose and slipped from around his neck. He let it drop through his fingers; it fell to the floor without even a whisper. He put the tips of his fingers to James' cheek next. James leaned into them, noticing the way two were rough and two were smooth. Gabe must have been chewing on them again.

He reached up and pulled on Gabe's tie. It slid from its knot more easily than his had. The silk was cool on the ends and warm where it had gone around Gabe's neck. He let it drop from his fingers as well.

Gabe took a few steps back, and James followed as if being led in a dance. And he followed where Gabe led. It was so easy and felt so right. He usually avoided the easy path. Easy was usually wrong.

Gabe changed directions, moving quickly behind James and slipping his coat from his body. James shivered at the sudden change in temperature, from being wrapped in the sultry jacket to having only the fine linen shirt between his body and the air.

The chill left as quickly as it had arrived. Gabe stepped in close, pressing himself to James' back, putting out a powerful heat. He leaned back, still feeling like he was in a dance that had no music with a rhythm that was in constant flux. But still Gabe led perfectly.

Gabe stripped off his own jacket without ever taking his chest from James' body. He let the jacket drop to the floor, not even bothering to toss it toward the hooks as he had with James'.

He pressed his lips to James' neck, right above his collar. James felt his toes curl and his body tingle. Gabe's fingers were back, skimming along his cheek, and his thumb brushed across James' lips. He flicked out his tongue to tickle it.

Gabe exhaled long and slow, his warm breath slipping under James' collar. His fingers left James' face and went instead to his throat, popping open the high collar buttons. James let out a long breath, unaware of just how constricted he had felt until that moment.

Gabe slid around him until they were once again face-to-face. He thought they might kiss, but instead Gabe just looked at him, eyes dark in the dim light. He felt his breath hitch and that tightening in his chest return. It was so much like the way Gabe had looked at him their first night. All those months ago now, standing so close that James had been able to smell the hint of peppers on his skin.

Now Gabe smelled faintly of fancy cologne that had nearly worn away.

He took Gabe's hand and laced their fingers together as if they would dance. Gabe took his other hand, lifted it, and kissed his palm. James closed his eyes and nearly fell forward. Gabe kissed the heel of his palm next and then placed a kiss on the inside of his wrist. James whimpered softly. Somehow those three small kisses had his head spinning with greater pleasure than kisses in far more intimate areas.

Gabe stepped backward, leading them with just the knowledge of the dimensions of his own home.

He didn't lead them to the bedroom, but rather to the large couch of cool leather draped with blankets of the same spun and woven silk as the one on Gabe's bed. He sat on them and drew James onto his lap, giving James the height advantage for once.

James took it, tilting Gabe's head back and into a slow, lazy kiss, their tongues just flitting around each other's, chasing the ghost flavor of champagne. Gabe's arms went around his body, pulling him close. James' fingers went into Gabe's hair, tangling themselves in the dark curls, destroying the last of the control imposed by handfuls of hair gel that smelled slightly of mint and clashed with the cologne.

Gabe sighed into the kiss and held James tight.

He and Gabe kissed. He didn't think about time; he didn't think about anything beyond the feel of Gabe's arms around him and the taste of Gabe on his lips, the sound of their tiny moans and sighs in his ears.

At some point Gabe pulled away from the kiss and took a deep breath. He leaned in, laying his head against James' chest. James became aware of his own heart pounding strong and steady. Gabe looked up at him, a small soft smile on his lips. James kissed those lips, then stood. Gabe followed.

This time James took Gabe's hand and led the dance toward the bedroom. There was no rush. He was content to keep kissing if that was all the night had in store, but he wanted to be lying down in Gabe's arms while it happened.

Gabe halted them at the foot of the bed. His fingers went to James' shirt, carefully releasing each button until it hung loose from his shoulders. James granted him the same favor, tracing his fingers across Gabe's chest as he went. When he was done, he leaned in and put a kiss on Gabe's collarbone, right over the lump where it had cracked in a car crash long before they'd met.

Gabe stroked his head and whispered something into his hair that he couldn't make out. Gabe finished stripping their shirts from their bodies, letting them drop to the floor.

James wanted to speak. He wanted to ask what Gabe wanted next, but he didn't want to break the silence between them. It felt too important. Suddenly Gabe dropped to his knees and began to untie the laces of James' shoes. He grinned up at James, and James grinned back. Gabe pulled the shoes from his feet, then his socks. Then he pressed his thumbs against the arch of his left foot. James sat hard on the bed as his legs gave out. Gabe rubbed harder, and James' head swam. He collapsed backward, his moan merging with Gabe's chuckle to break the silence.

Gabe's hands left his feet, and he heard the rustle of clothing. He raised his head to look at Gabe, standing still and bare at the foot of the bed. In the dim light, the trim lines of Gabe's body stood out in sharp contrast. He looked almost unreal, except for the steady rise and fall of his chest and his heavy gaze. James felt like he couldn't move under the weight of Gabe's eyes.

Finally, Gabe smiled and stripped the last of James' clothes from his body.

He scooted back, letting Gabe crawl up and over him. Gabe stopped halfway, putting a soothing kiss over the old burn scar that still marked James' thigh. From there he continued to kiss his way up James' body, each kiss warm and wet. He squirmed under Gabe's kisses and caresses but didn't demand more. Gabe put a kiss in the hollow of his throat before pushing himself up and looking into James' eyes. Gabe's eyes were black in the light and unreadable, but Gabe took a breath. He stroked his hand over James' hair.

"Oh," Gabe whispered softly, shattering the silence between them.

Before James could say anything, Gabe's mouth was on his again, this time strong and demanding. He probed with his tongue and nipped at James' lips. He ran his hands quick and sure across James' body. James thrashed beneath him but not to escape. He kissed back with as much passion as Gabe was pouring into him. Something had changed. Each touch was burning, and each kiss felt like it was designed to steal the air from his lungs.

Gabe pressed his face into the curve of James' neck. He licked and nipped the spot. "Oh, James," he growled, pushing the force of his words into James' skin.

James whimpered, his eyes shut tight, his other senses overloading at Gabe's onslaught. Gabe ground his hips down against James' body. "Do you feel this?" he whispered. "Do you feel how much I want you?"

James nodded. He couldn't speak, only pant for breath as Gabe slid a hand between them and reclaimed his mouth. James bucked hard into the touch, his control ragged at best, but he couldn't even begin to analyze Gabe's sudden shift. He could barely think at all. His mind was linked solely to the places where Gabe's skin was pressed against his. Those places burned.

Gabe yanked himself back, and James' whole body jerked up to follow. Gabe grabbed him roughly, and soon James had his legs wrapped around Gabe's waist, their bodies squeezed tight, and their tongues tangled around each other.

Gabe shoved a hand between their bodies as James held on tight, nearly afraid to let go, but soon even that thought was gone as he became a creature of pure sensation that was clawing desperately for release.

Gabe beat him to it, roaring out his name, but he didn't stop, his hand still working between their bodies.

"More," James managed to gasp out, his fiery edge still just out of reach. Gabe gave him more. He stroked James hard and fast, crushing their lips together. It was enough. A scream pulled its way from James' body as his last shred of control gave way. He jerked and shuddered, and Gabe kept stroking him. He sobbed out Gabe's name as the final shock hit, his body finally collapsing, his limbs heavy, and his lungs burning. The only sound he could hear was his own pulse.

Gabe collapsed next to him. He reached up, and with rough coordination, ran his thumb across James' lips. James kissed it. Gabe gave a sweet, sleepy smile, closed his eyes, and drifted off.

For once James didn't. He watched as Gabe's breathing became soft and slow. Usually it was the other way around,

James waking to Gabe's eyes on him. But James' brain was waking up and coming back online. Something had changed. Something in the way Gabe had looked at him, kissed him, ran his hands over his body. It was as if Gabe had suddenly wanted more of him, all of him, and James didn't know why or what it meant or if he had more to give.

He slid from under Gabe's arm, trying not to wake him. He should be trying to sleep, the most restful nights in his life having occurred in Gabe's bed, but the inside of his head wouldn't settle down. He grabbed the blue robe that hung by Gabe's closet. Somewhere along the way, it had become James' robe when he stayed over.

As quietly as he could, he padded his way across the apartment and out of the french doors. It was cool as he settled himself onto the swing, looking out into the night. It wasn't much of a view from that side of the building. Lights of neatly laid-out suburbs were sliced apart by snaking freeways and surrounded by office blocks and industrial parks. Every so often a patch of black indicated a piece of parkland.

He thought about a house with a view of the ocean. He thought about a swing on a porch with that view and a storm coming in the distance, like the seascape paintings that adorned Gabe's walls. He gave himself a mental slap; that had become instinctive over the years when his mind started slipping toward the impossible and unattainable. He dragged his mind to his monthly budget, something painfully solid and real. He started shifting pennies around in his head to pay for Dylan's last physiotherapy appointment. It was like financial solitaire or Tetris. He made a mental note to call his mother, who had offered to help out with Dylan's birthday party.

He turned around at the sound of the french doors opening. Gabe stepped out, dressed in his dark charcoal sleep pants. "I'm sorry, did I wake you up?"

"No." Gabe sat down next to him. "Are you okay?"

"I'm fine," James replied automatically. "Couldn't sleep. Thought I'd get some air, think about stuff."

Gabe shifted close. "Anything I can help out with?"

He shook his head. "No. I'm fine, just work and Dylan. He's got prom next week, and I need to remember to call my mother. We're planning his graduation slash birthday party."

"Having a big blowout?"

"Not really, he actually asked for something low-key. Ever been up to Tilden Park?"

"Sure, we used to take school field trips there. They've got that minifarm and weird little nature museum."

"There's also a picnic area and a big antique carousel. I used to take Dylan there when he was little, if he was good. It was only fifty cents a ride, but I'd make a big deal out of buying the ticket and letting him pick which horse he wanted."

"Which one did he like best?"

"There was this gray one. It wasn't a fancy one, and there were a few like it, but he always went for this one particular gray horse. Never could figure out why." James felt his throat close up. He could still hear the carousel tune banged out by an old animatronic band and see Dylan gripping tight to the twisted brass pole of his favorite horse.

"You know he's not going that far? Stanford's an hour from you if the traffic isn't too bad. Twenty minutes from here."

"I know. That's what he keeps telling me too." James rubbed his face. "I'm sorry. I should let you sleep."

"Don't be. What else is going on in your head?"

"Just... nothing," James lied. "Nothing interesting." He didn't have words for everything that was going on in his head or twisting around his body. The way his body turned toward Gabe the moment he stepped onto the porch. The strange way his chest and throat kept getting tight when Gabe told him he was smart or attractive. He couldn't even explain to himself the urge he had to lean over the edge of the building and just scream his throat raw until the whole Bay was awake with him.

Gabe put his arms around him. James closed his eyes. It had felt wonderful the first time Gabe held him on that little bridge at the country club, and each time after that was different, but as good if not better. And each time it happened, James felt himself slide deeper into Gabe's warmth and peace.

"Do you think you'll ever get around to building yourself a house?" he asked.

"I hope so. I think so. I don't want to be an old man puttering around this place. Rather be an old man puttering around someplace that I built and designed. Why?"

"No reason."

Gabe didn't reply. He just set the swing to slowly rock. "Every time I sit out here now I think of us and chocolate pudding." James smiled, then suddenly yawned. A second later Gabe yawned as well. "Okay. Maybe we should go back to bed."

"In a minute," James mumbled. He was enjoying the contrast of the cool air and Gabe's warm body pressed against his.

Gabe pulled him tighter. "Okay. We still have plenty of time before morning."

9

Gabe watched the slow rise and fall of James' chest. It was obvious James had been lying when he said everything was fine and that he wasn't thinking about anything important. The small hitch in his voice was always the giveaway. He wished James would tell him whatever was wrong, especially if it was something between the two of them that had him bothered.

He brushed aside a stray bit of hair that had fallen across James' face. In the faint light, he could see the outline of James' features. He smiled into the dark. He had felt it that night, a squeeze in his chest, and something locked into place in his mind. It had been building for a long time, but now it was at a point where it couldn't be ignored or mistaken for anything else. It was love. Clean, bright, and fully formed, like a star first bursting into life. He'd wanted to tell James the very second he clued in, holding himself over James' body, looking down into his eyes. He'd been told by many that declarations of love midsex don't count, but that hadn't stopped the sudden and overwhelming need to confess his heart.

He would have to tread carefully. James could very well bolt at a grand declaration of love, and Gabe still needed to get a solid handle on exactly what he was feeling before he could. But there would be a time, soon, when he would be able to say it to James, and if he was lucky, James just might say it back.

And maybe after that, James would let him in. Maybe he would share the worries that woke him in the middle of the night and start accepting some of the nicer things Gabe wanted to give him.

James muttered in his sleep while his eyes fluttered about under the lids. A frown came across his sleeping face. Gabe gave him a squeeze. "It's all okay," he whispered.

James shifted a bit but still slept.

He let his own mind wander to idle fantasies of love immortal. It was something he hadn't done since he was much younger and far more foolish. Usually when he looked into the future, it was full of meetings and product releases for technology that hadn't even been conceived of yet. If there was anyone else in those images of the future, it was Frank and Nate, Margaret, and maybe Sarah or Harry's kids, if they have any. There was no one just for him.

If he had time to go to a therapist, he was sure they'd have a lot to say on that. As it stood now, things were changing rapidly. His mind was racing ahead, tracing out possible futures. The one he was clinging to had James by his side. It had a home that looked out over the ocean instead of a tangle of freeways. It had vacations and slow Sunday breakfasts. It had Dylan's kids rushing around, calling him Grandpa.

Gabe yanked his thoughts up fast and hard. Thinking about grandchildren before even saying "I love you" was rushing too far and fast ahead. If his car crash all those years ago had taught him anything, it was that going too fast was a good way for everyone involved to get hurt.

He took a deep breath and wrapped himself around James. He would be careful; he would keep to the pace James set, not add extra pressure. It wasn't like he didn't have a million and one other things to consider. After all, the Russians were coming.

IN THE MORNING when the sun started to arc over the Bay, burning off the fog, Gabe was still in love. When his phone started pinging at him to tell him he had a dozen urgent messages, he was still in love. When James got up, wrapped himself in that sexy blue robe, wandered into the kitchen and returned with two cups of coffee, Gabe very nearly proposed on the spot.

He took a sip of coffee, excused himself from the particular phone call he was on, and gave James a long, slow, dirty kiss that tasted of sweet coffee. He leaned back and pulled James close to him. "I could do this forever, you know?"

"Do what?"

"This. Wake up next to you, have you bring me coffee, then I pull you back to bed."

"You would get bored of me."

"No, I wouldn't." He kissed James again and ran his hands across any bit of skin he had access to. He wanted to relearn James' body through this new filter of love. "Tell me you don't have anything to do today."

"Not really. Baseball is over, Dylan is mainly just studying and working on papers, the laundry can hold off for a day."

"Good." He wrapped his arms around James' body and squeezed tight until James gave a little cough. "Sorry. I really do wish we could do this forever."

"If we stayed here doing this, that might put a dent in your trying to save the world."

"I'll just send a memo to Tam. She'll take care of it."

"I have no doubt of that."

"Tam, staying in bed with my boyfriend for the next year or

two. Please remind me to pick up a Father's Day present, and save the world while you're out."

James laughed, then kissed Gabe again and didn't stop for quite some time.

GABE WHISTLED as he bounced into the office on Monday morning, despite some lingering tiredness. He'd managed to ignore or deflect a sizable amount of work and kept James in bed for a good deal of Sunday, driving him home only late Sunday night.

He'd skimmed through the gossip blogs. There were several very good pictures of him and James. James' last name was still spelled wrong, and they were still claiming he was a professor, and there were still rumors about wedding bells, but that bit of false reporting annoyed him far less than it had the first time.

Nate and Frank slinked into his office, looking amused with themselves. "Did you see the gossip pages this morning?"

"Yes."

"Then when are the wedding bells?"

Gabe shrugged and changed his desktop background to a photo of him and James dancing close.

"Wait a second." Frank squinted at him. "That wasn't a denial. That wasn't even an eye roll. You're not actually engaged, are you?"

Gabe did give them an eye roll this time. "Do you think I'd get engaged and not tell you two first?"

"Yes," they answered in unison, then Frank nudged Nate. "Look at that face of his."

"Oh my God. We haven't seen that face in a long, long time."

"You see my face every damn day."

"Not that particular face." Frank reached across the desk and tried to pinch his cheeks. "That is your 'I'm in love' face."

Gabe batted Frank's hand away while trying to frown but failed at that. "It's none of your business."

Both Frank and Nate giggled, sounding like a couple of teenaged girls. "For the record, we approve of this development," Frank stated primly. "Have you told him yet?"

This time Gabe did frown and tried to look like he was focusing on the documents in front of him. "I'd rather not send him running screaming into the night."

"Oh no. You need to tell him. He needs to know where he stands. Listen to the guy who's already screwed up two marriages and is not putting money on his third. You need to be honest with your feelings. All of them. Good, bad, or otherwise."

Gabe looked up at Frank. Frank didn't discuss his interpersonal failings often. He was the playboy of the three of them. He and Nate just rolled with it and made sure there were mountains of legal documents that kept Frank's third of the company in Frank's control only, no matter what. They actually all had documents keeping the company just between the three of them. It was the TechPrim tripod.

"He's…. He's very new to the whole relationship thing. I don't want him to feel pressured into saying something he doesn't mean."

Frank stretched his long torso over Gabe's desk until they were nose to nose. "You are an idiot. He is really into you. Tell him."

———

THE PICTURE TAPED OVER JAMES' monitor had been taken at some point when he and Gabe were dancing. Their hands were clasped together, and their bodies pressed close. Perhaps closer than was really appropriate for the situation. James' head was tilted up ever so slightly, and Gabe was looking down at him.

Their lips were just a few inches apart. It was, all told, a pretty good picture of the two of them, but someone had written across the top 'Can I Haz a Kiss?' James sighed, pulled the picture off his monitor, and cleared his throat loudly, keeping his face grim.

"This is unacceptable." He held up the picture. "I will not allow such things in my work area." He watched everyone on his team squirm. "I refuse to allow this bastardization of spelling and grammar in my department. The English language is a lovely thing, and I do not appreciate its mistreatment in this manner. Am I clear?"

Everyone nodded seriously while trying to smother smiles.

"Good."

James sat down and set the picture carefully aside. He checked his e-mail. Then, thinking on it, he pulled out his phone and took a picture of the picture.

My team left this for me. I yelled at them about the bad grammar and spelling.

He sent the picture and the message to Gabe.

A minute later his phone pinged, and he opened a picture file from Gabe. In it Gabe was making a silly kissy face to the camera. James laughed, felt that squeeze in his chest, then set about figuring out how to make it the notice image for calls from Gabe.

Russian property law is still boring and confusing. Would much rather be making out with you. Miss you.

James looked down at the text message. It was just a stupid little text, but there had been that same squeeze in his chest, hard and tight. For a moment he could barely breathe. He was pretty sure he knew why, but his mind skittered around the thought, looking for another explanation. Any other explanation. He paced his living room, feeling claustrophobic. He was tempted to go running or something, except he'd never gone running in his adult life, so instead he was bouncing off his own walls.

Dylan called out from the kitchen. "You know I can hear you pacing out there. Whatever it is, you need to chill."

James stepped into the kitchen to possibly grumble at Dylan about telling his father to chill. Dylan was hunched over a book, and it hardly seemed worth it. "Can I ask you a question?" James regretted the words the second they came out of his mouth, but he had to ask someone. He could ask the ladies, but he wasn't up for another round of building gossip.

He already knew it would be less a question and more of a confirmation.

"Sure." Dylan didn't look up from his book.

"I mean a serious one because I've got no one else to ask, and our relationship is just way too backward some days."

Dylan set the book aside. "Shoot."

James froze. He looked down at his son, his sweet baby boy, and just couldn't speak. The level of wrong in the conversation was just too high, and the level of fear was higher still.

"You know what, never mind." James turned to head to his room. Maybe an early night, a very early night, was what he needed.

"Oh no." Dylan jumped up, rushed ahead of him, and easily blocked the hallway. "You don't get to walk out after an opening like that."

James dropped his face into his hands. "I can't do this," he muttered.

"Do what?"

He closed his eyes and tried to imagine he was talking to just about anyone other than Dylan because he needed someone to tell him what was going on before he just started screaming.

"Is there a moment," he started carefully. "When you've been with someone for a little while, when it suddenly feels different?"

"Define different."

"I don't know…. Like asthma, or a heart attack, or some bit of your brain just starts going funny and thinking about different things it didn't think about before?"

Dylan tipped his head and squinted at him. James felt like a bug under a magnifying glass. "That sounds more like something you should go to a doctor for."

"Great, yes, thank you, must be asthma, step aside."

"Nope." Dylan folded his arms and peered down at his father. "Tell me, do these funny mini–heart attacks and brain cramps only happen when Gabe's around?" James didn't answer. "And there's a weird kind of twitch behind your eyes and some part of your brain is locked into some other part of your brain that you didn't even know was there before but it just likes to run off on its own?"

James started to fold in on himself.

"Dad." Dylan crouched down so he could look his father in the eye. "You're an idiot. It's called being in love. Massively, head over heels, painfully in love, and I'm pretty sure you knew that already."

James *had* known that of course, deep down. There really was no other explanation, but that knowledge was not making the experience any more pleasant. "Fuck." He sat down on the couch, planting his face firmly back into his hands. He'd been in love, once, maybe, at age fourteen, with Benjamin Steven. That had ended less than well, and they'd been hardly more than children at the time. That was the sum total of his relationship with love. Dylan sat beside him, the couch sagging and creaking under his size.

"Every time Catherine smiles at me, it's like someone has reached down my throat, grabbed each lung, and is using them to squeeze my heart. Been like that since we were seven. It is the worst fucking thing on earth, and I never want it to go away."

Dylan's voice was full of sympathy. James wanted to cry, scream, and laugh all at once. For some reason his teeth hurt. "What the fuck do I do now?"

"I suggest calling up your really great boyfriend, who is actually majorly into you, and setting up another date, and when it feels right, tell him you love him."

"Right. 'Hi, Gabe, I'm thirty-two, you were my first, I wouldn't know a proper relationship from a hole in the ground, but I'm pretty sure I'm in love with you. How's your day going?'"

"I'd phrase it better."

"And then what?" A full awareness of what his love would mean pressed down on him. It was hard to breathe again. "He's the head of a multinational, multibillion-dollar… kingdom. He does not need some…. He does not need me dropping all this on him."

"You watch way too many telenovelas, and what's to say he isn't madly in love with you?"

A headache flared up right behind his eyeballs. "I'm going to bed."

"It's seven in the evening."

"Then I'll get plenty of sleep."

"Dad—"

"No. I can't… I just can't." James pushed past his son and into his barren little room. He flopped onto his bed, not even bothering to undress. He hadn't changed his pillowcase since the last time Gabe had come over, and it smelled like Gabe's hair gel and green-tea shampoo.

He hadn't changed that pillowcase specifically because he liked the smell. It felt relaxing, warm, and safe. He rested when he was enveloped by it. Usually. Now it just reminded him of something he was trying to push away.

He growled, tried breathing through his mouth instead, and attempted to sleep.

JAMES POKED at his chili verde. Gabe had made the lunchtime trip north, and they were tucked into the corner of a little Mexican place off of Shattuck. The food was good, but it had been almost a week since they'd seen each other face to face. James thought that would be enough time to rein in his emotions. But as soon as Gabe had stepped out of his car, James felt the breath drawn from his body. He wanted to throw himself at Gabe, to whisper in his ear and hear very specific words whispered back. It hurt.

"Is everything okay?"

James' head snapped up, a smile jumping to his lips. "What? Yes, everything's fine."

"Are you sure? Is the food okay?"

"It's good." James proved it by taking a bite. "I'm just thinking too much again. Dylan's prom is tomorrow," he added, since it technically was something he was thinking about, a bit, at least.

Gabe smiled. "Is he excited?"

"He's pretending not to be, but he cleaned out the car and spent a half hour in front of the mirror yesterday trying out new ways of combing his hair."

"And how are you?"

"Trying not to panic. Mrs. Serrano and Mrs. Avila have their girls going to prom as well, so the three of us are going to get together, drink coffee with a little too much rum in it, and pretend like we're not feeling old."

"You are nowhere near old, and you know it."

That didn't mean James wasn't feeling old. "His graduation is just a couple of weeks away as well. His birthday too. I need to work on organizing his party. I need to get him his present."

"What are you getting him?"

"I'm thinking about getting him a watch. I've been putting some money to the side. I know he could really use a new computer, but I don't think I could swing that, and... I don't know, it's a little old-fashioned, but a watch feels like something a father should get his son for his eighteenth."

"I think that's a good idea."

"Thanks."

"Would you mind if I upgraded his system as a gift? I mean, I think his laptop is running off of whale oil or something."

James pushed down his kneejerk reaction of saying "No thank you. I can handle it." Dylan really did need a new laptop, and Gabe *was* asking if it was okay. "I think he'd appreciate that very much, and I'm sure you're invited to the party." Gabe smiled at him, and James felt his chest tighten until it was almost hard to breathe.

"Just tell me when. How are things at work for you?"

James didn't particularly want to talk about work. The end of the school year always left a twitch in the corner of his left eye. "Not the best time of year. Half my staff is begging for extra time off so they can finish their projects for the year—the ones they've had months to work on. And the entire campus flips out if there's so much as a glitch anywhere in the network because everyone is trying to finish their projects for the year. And half my staff is graduating, and I need to start looking for their replacements preferably before September so I can get them trained up before the big rush."

"I'm sure you'll be able to find some good people."

There were always people who needed work, and James had been through the cycle enough times to know that. It didn't make the whole thing less irritating. "On the upside, Dave managed to successfully take a message the other day."

"That is progress, indeed."

"How are things going with the Great Endeavor?" James asked, desperate to change the topic.

"Ramping up. Russians are showing up in a couple of weeks for the next phase of negotiations. And the last of the Solar Flare team has been moved into the main campus labs. I don't know how they got any work done in their old offices. They would have probably been better equipped in someone's garage."

"I'm sure they'll appreciate it."

"I saw one hug their dedicated in-lab server. And I even got to go down and hand them their revised contracts." Gabe looked incredibly pleased with himself.

"I can't picture the dean hand delivering the IT contracts."

"Any time I can give someone a job or let them keep one they have, it's a good thing. First time I had to fire some people, it was because I'd miscalculated our resource needs in our fourth year and overhired. I felt like the biggest asshole on the planet. Like I was putting a gun to someone's head and saying, 'Hey, good luck making the rent, hope your kid doesn't need fillings this month.' I swore I'd never do that again."

James had nothing to say except for the three words that still sat on the edge of his lips. If he'd heard something like that from anyone else, he'd have thought it was a half-truth if not a full-out lie. But he'd seen Gabe with his employees, the way he had shook each hand and knew each name, and had listened with honest interest. His employees were TechPrim, and TechPrim was his baby, his grand creation. Out to make the world a better place one solar cell and insurance plan at a time. For a moment James was sure he was going to stop breathing. He settled his hand over Gabe's and gave it a squeeze. "I'm sure you're still racking up a lot of good Karma."

DYLAN'S TIE was a deep blue, the same color as Catherine's hair tips. It was a pretied clip-on, which saved James and Dylan a second round of trying to figure out how to tie a bow tie. James straightened it a little.

"Well, Dad, how do I look?" He gave a quick turn in front of the mirror in James' room.

James took a step back and looked his son over. "You look very grown-up." Dylan rolled his eyes. "I mean it." It had taken three stops but they had found a tux that wasn't too tight and didn't make him look like a linebacker. The dark blue waistcoat brought out his eyes, and the slicked-back hairstyle he'd finally gone with made him look more like a junior executive than a high school senior. He looked like he could have slipped into the TechPrim prom without any questions.

There was a knock on the door, and Dylan nearly jumped out of his skin and began hyperventilating.

"I'll go get it for you. Take a couple of deep breaths."

When James opened the front door, his jaw dropped. Catherine was in a sleeveless gown of deep blue, constructed of satin and layers of bias-cut organza that draped down from just below her breasts and brushed the floor. It had to have been either expensive as hell or a pain in the ass to make (and he wished he didn't know as much about dressmaking as he did, but he'd helped hem one-too-many quinceañera and bridesmaid's dresses). Her face was done up with far less makeup than usual, and there were small white flowers woven into her short hair.

"Wow." She rolled her eyes. James stepped aside and let her in. "That is a very nice dress."

Catherine shifted around. "I never wear dresses. This feels so weird." She grabbed the top of her dress and yanked up. "And I'm afraid it's going to slip off."

"Turn around, and raise your hands over your head." She squinted at him suspiciously. "Seriously."

She slowly turned and raised her arms up. James pinched the top edge of the dress and gave it a good shake, then quickly ran his hand down the sides of the zipper. "You've got a stack of rigilene sewn into the bodice. It's not going anywhere."

Catherine lowered her arms. "And since when do you know anything about dresses?"

"Don't ask."

Catherine was still shifting the dress around when Dylan finally emerged from the hall. "Hi." His voice was barely a whisper. He was swallowing hard and looked about to faint. James felt a moment of true pity for his son. "You look really nice."

Catherine looked shyly away. "You look nice too."

"Thanks."

"Okay." James clapped his hands together before things could get any more uncomfortable. "You two stand together so I can get pictures."

They slid shyly together, hip to hip, like they were afraid to touch and hadn't wrestled in the sand as children. James pulled out his phone. "And smile." He took a photo. It was perfect. "And one more." He took picture after picture, fiddling with flash, filters, and settings until they were over the sudden shyness and rolling their eyes in unison.

"Enough, Dad. We don't want to be late."

"Okay. Have a good time, you two. Be good. Drive carefully. Call me if you get in any trouble."

"We'll be fine."

James gave Dylan a quick hug and tried to ignore how fast his own heart was beating. He gave Catherine a quick squeeze as well, being careful not to step on her dress. "Have fun."

Dylan put a hand gently on the small of her back and led Catherine out the door. It closed with a loud click just as the fan in the fridge ground to a halt. Suddenly the only sound in the apartment was the stuttering second hand on the kitchen clock. James took a deep breath and went to find some coffee and rum.

JAMES WAS into his second coffee and rum and feeling lightly buzzed when a message came in from Gabe.

How are you doing? Did Dylan get away okay?

Dylan looks all grown up now. I'm OK. Coffee and Rum helps.

:-) Wish I was up there with you. You're cute when you're tipsy. Homework night for me. I'm glad I've got Tam and all those lawyers because this is eating my brain. How hard can it be to buy one bankrupt company? No good deed....

Wish you were here too.

James gulped down some more coffee.

Homework first.

11

THIS NIGHTMARE had been coming for months, and Tamyra had been reminding him every day for a week, but he'd buried the threat under thoughts of James in bed and Russian mineral rights.

Gabe was now wishing he'd taken his migraine medication while the studio lights baked down on him and the makeup made his skin itch. Some right-wing talking-head puppet from one of TechPrim's minor competitors was trying to bait him from another studio in New York. Gabe never understood why he had to do these interviews, if they could even be called that. TechPrim wasn't publicly traded and never would be, they dominated several different markets and were major players in many others, they could buy and sell US Senators, even though they refrained from doing so, and they were ranked as one of the best companies to work for globally.

But someone, somewhere, thought it would be a good idea to put him on TV and argue business with some asshole. He always managed to block out what a complete nightmare they were to the point where he would agree to do them again. At least it wasn't FOX this time.

Gabe leaned in toward the cameras. "You lost millions of dollars last winter when your employees and their families got the flu. I spent a few hundred grand to vaccinate all TechPrim employees and their families and saved billions. That's not socialism. It's good business sense and being a decent boss. And considering the fact that we posted a 5.8 percent profit jump last quarter and you posted a 7.9 percent drop, I think I might be on to something."

Some other talking head from DC popped up and started ranting about tax rates and job creation. Gabe drove his nails into his palms and fought down the urge to just say "I'm right, you're wrong, suck it." Instead he nodded like he actually cared.

JAMES CRAWLED out from under a desk, banging his shoulder in the process. There was something strange about the economics department. They always managed to mess up their hardware in complicated ways that no other department could manage. This time it was a router that was throwing an absolute tantrum; he would have to replace it. Normally he'd send Martin, but Martin had begged for a half day off to go to his sister's thesis defense, and just now he was feeling that he was way too soft on his employees.

He shook the router at the elderly professor who'd called him down. "If I crack this open and find soda or coffee or anything sticky inside, I'm making sure it comes out of your department's budget."

"I'm sure none of our students—"

"Who said anything about students?" James had moved beyond being deferential to tenure. This one looked like he could be dead before fall semester started. "They've been practically surgically attached to a computer since birth; they know better. They're not the ones who think you can just spill a smoothie on a piece of hardware, mop up the outside, and not worry about it." The professor tried to give him the "I have tenure and a PhD" glare, but James just wasn't in the mood. He was still feeling weird about everything else in his life right now. He looked over the professor's shoulder to where a TV was on, muted. It was some business cable channel with a bunch of talking heads, and then suddenly Gabe was full screen. He didn't look happy.

"Hey, could you turn that up?" James asked.

"What?"

James just grabbed the remote off the desk and unmuted it.

"...responsibilities, and not to shareholders. I have a duty to my employees, to give them a safe and healthy environment. One where they can be proud of the work they do for an honest wage. To make sure they know their hard work has value. I have a responsibility to our customers to guarantee they always receive the best quality product and service in exchange for money they gained through their own hard work. I have a responsibility to myself and to my partners to work tirelessly to help maintain a company I am damn proud of, and that work takes priority. It certainly takes priority over sitting here arguing with people who are letting their own companies burn."

"Yes, well." The moderator quickly jumped in as all the other talking heads began to yell.

The professor shook his head, his lips pinched tight. "If that man would just—"

"Don't." James raised one finger. His heart was pounding even as the program cut to their next segment. Gabe's words were ringing in his ears.

"I was just saying—"

"No. Gabriel Juarez is my boyfriend, so just don't."

JAMES WONDERED JUST what percentage of his life he spent crawling around on the floor trying to fix or find things. Or in this case, trying to clean out the back of Dylan's closet. Over the years boxes of papers had been shoved back there, and at least one contained Dylan's vaccination records. He hoped. They should have been in the folder with Dylan's report cards and transcripts.

He opened the oldest-looking of the boxes. The crayon drawing of a house that was carefully labeled Room 103 1st Grade was a good sign he was on the right track. He removed each piece of yellowing paper carefully. There were drawings, spelling tests, worksheets of addition and subtraction, a brown and orange handprint turkey.

He unfolded a sheet of yellow legal paper and found his own handwriting.

It is my duty as a parent to always prioritize the well-being of my child and that includes ensuring the quality of his education.

James dropped his face into his hand. *Shit.* It was his PTA speech. He'd actually run for a place on the PTA board after learning that the school was considering shifting from a phonics-based to a whole-language reading program without consulting the parents. He'd been all of twenty. *What was I thinking?* It was obvious what he had been thinking. It was right there in the speech. Duty, responsibility, priority, and a desire to be taken seriously. The mantras of his life. He hadn't been taken seriously. He found out later that he'd gotten all of two votes. One was his own; he never found out who cast the other. And the school changed to a whole-language reading program. He still blamed it for some poor spelling results in middle school.

James' phone rang with Gabe's stupid kissy face on the screen. He felt his whole mood lift as he answered. "Hello."

"Hey there." Gabe sounded breathless, as if he had been running. "How are you doing?"

"I'm fine, digging through old boxes. How are you?"

Gabe took a deep breath. "Still running between meetings. Thought I'd take a moment to call, see how you're doing."

James' chest gave that little squeeze that sent an ache through him but also put a smile on his face. He glanced up at Dylan's alarm clock; it was almost seven.

There was a voice in the background of the call before James could reply. "We're already an hour and a half late." Gabe's voice was muffled but still understandable. "Two more minutes isn't going to matter at this point." There was a different voice in the background. "Sorry," Gabe said into the phone, this time sounding tired. "Can I call you tonight?"

"Of course. But you should probably sleep instead."

"What's the old saying? I'll sleep when I'm dead? I'll try to shove around some things later in the week. Maybe we can grab lunch or something."

"Sure."

There was a voice in the background again. "Sorry, I've got to go. Bye."

"Bye." The line went dead, and James felt his mood slip, which annoyed him more than anything else. His speech was still in his other hand. He read it over again. In retrospect it was maybe a little aggressive, but it got across his feelings on the matter, loud and clear.

A FLAMENCO REMIX OF "HOTEL CALIFORNIA" filtered into James' dream before waking him. He fumbled for his phone.

"Gabe?" he mumbled, squinting at his alarm clock, the digital numbers seeming far too bright. It was 3:18 a.m.

"What?" he heard Gabe mumble.

"Gabe?"

"James?" Gabe sounded confused.

"Yes, you called me." James wondered if Gabe was drunk again. It didn't quite sound like it, though.

"Oh. Oh, yeah, I was just going to text you before I went to sleep. I must have hit the wrong button." Gabe's words began to fade out toward the end of the sentence.

"You're just now getting to bed?"

"Had work to do. Wanted to call you earlier but…." Gabe trailed off, but James stayed silent. Over the phone he could hear Gabe's soft breathing. He wondered if Gabe was already in bed or if he was slumped over his kitchen table where he liked to work. He'd once told James that he didn't have a home office so he'd be less likely to bring work home with him. Both he and James had laughed.

He heard a soft beeping over the line; it meant another call was coming in. He should wake Gabe up, tell him about the call. Three in the morning, finally heading to bed, and someone was trying to call him.

Wake up. The words were right there on James' lips. *Wake up, you have work.* But it was the middle of the night, and Gabe had called him, not whoever was on the other line. Between the beeps he could hear Gabe breathe, slow and deep. He loved that sound. He loved to sleep to the sound of Gabe breathing. Whoever was calling obviously didn't know what they were interrupting or most likely didn't care.

The beeping stopped. James felt guilty. It might have been important. It could have been about any one of a hundred things all over the world that Gabe needed to keep a finger on. And James had let Gabe sleep. James hadn't said a word so he could listen to Gabe sleep.

"Gabe." The word came out in a choked whisper. He didn't want to wake Gabe up. He also didn't want him to spend what was left of the night slumped and twisted over paperwork.

"Gabe." He raised his voice just a hair. This time he got a slight hum in response.

"Gabe, are you in bed?" There was another hum that sounded like a positive response. "Okay." There was a beeping again, over Gabe's breathing. James dug his nails into his palm, shoved down the guilt as hard as he could, and for a few more minutes let himself listen to Gabe sleep.

12

Gabe was rolling in a mix of guilty and happy. Guilty because he hadn't been able to see James for a week and happy because James was sitting across from him now eating a spring roll. He had made it a point to text James at least once a day. He didn't want James to think for one second that he wasn't a priority in Gabe's life, and he did his best to apologize regularly for his negligence.

Truthfully he shouldn't even be having lunch right now, but he'd rebelled against his own timeline, sneaked out of a back door, and hopped in his car. It was only the memory of having road gravel picked out of his back that kept him from doing ninety in the center lane.

He reached across the table and put his hand over James'. James smiled, but there was something tentative about it. "How are you doing?'

"Fine. Counting down the days."

"Less than a week to go, isn't it?"

"Wednesday is graduation. Thursday is his birthday. Thursday afternoon is his party."

Shit, Gabe thought. "What time is the party?"

"Four thirty. They don't let you book the picnic ground too late in the day. Park closes at sunset anyway."

"I'll try to make it." Gabe had a bad feeling already that he wouldn't. "We have a meeting scheduled with the Russian lawyers on Thursday, but with any luck we'll get that day of negotiations knocked out early. I don't really know what there is to negotiate. We give them a few billion dollars, they give us a company. It shouldn't be this hard."

James gave another tentative smile. "Don't worry about it. If anything, Dylan will probably be jealous he's not in those meetings with you."

Gabe gave James' hand a squeeze. "Are you going to be okay? I know it's Dylan's birthday, but it's still a big day for you too."

James took a deep breath. "I'm going to be okay. He's not moving out for a few months yet. I can kind of slowly ease up on the death grip. I hope."

"I know all about death grips. The guys keep telling me I need to let go, but I think my hands have just sort of cramped up permanently around the company reins." James smiled that slightly off smile again, almost like he was scared and trying to hide it. "I'm sure Dylan will be fine. He's a smart kid and tough, and you've raised him right, and he's going to be a good and responsible adult. I'm sure of it."

"Thank you. I'll be fine."

"I know. I just worry sometimes."

James' face gave a strange little twitch, a flash of a frown. "So." James pulled his hand away. "When are the Russians coming?"

"They're flying in on Tuesday. We'll have meetings all day Wednesday and Thursday morning, and hopefully we'll hand everything off to the international lawyers to look over by Thursday lunch. Friday we'll be setting up for the third stage, and then there will be vodka, and if all goes well, in mid-

August I'll fly to Moscow to sign the last of the paperwork, spend the long winter getting staff and resources lined up, and we should be breaking ground in the spring. And with a lot of luck, by next summer I'll get to tell the Chinese mining industry to suck it. And within two Christmases some families in the Rust Belt will be a little merrier when we put some manufacturing plants online."

James smiled at him. It was a bright, beaming smile, but there was perhaps something a little sad around his eyes. Gabe was going to ask what was wrong again when his phone started to vibrate. "Shit." It was one of the international lawyers who was on his fifth round of fact checking. If he was calling on a weekend, it couldn't be good. "I'm sorry, I really need—"

"It's fine." James waved him toward the back of the restaurant even as Gabe was answering the phone.

"Hello." Gabe quickly found himself wishing he hadn't picked up the phone. Or that he had the same moral ambiguity of the assholes he'd argued with on national TV. Instead he found himself pressing his forehead against the wall in the back of a Thai restaurant because the son of the owner of a company he wanted to buy had been skimming off employee wages and threatening the employees with their jobs if they ever told. Half the money was in a Middle East slush fund that would be hard to get to, and the other half was in the bank accounts of various casinos, drug dealers, and prostitutes. He idly wondered if he could beat down his own sense of ethics long enough to take out a hit on the son. It would make things so much easier

In the end Gabe agreed that it would be best not to bother dealing with the police as it could delay the sale indefinitely. Instead they would put pressure on the owners to get the son out of the picture quickly and get the employees their stolen pay as part of a Christmas bonus or something. It would involve more negotiation, however.

Once Gabe hung up, he forced a smile onto his face and headed back to his table. He hoped the servers hadn't delayed the food. No reason for James to not eat because of a Russian with a drinking, drug, gambling, and sex problem.

Gabe's *tom kha gai* was waiting with James' *larb gai*.

"You should have started without me."

"It wasn't a bother. Everything okay?"

Gabe spooned some rice into his *tom kha*. "Every fresh round of due diligence turns up something new. We'll get there in the end."

James smiled. "I know you will."

Gabe did his best to keep up the conversation through lunch and not talk about work. It wasn't proving easy, not with his brain being all but eaten by international lawyers and Russian property law. And James—there was something up with James that he couldn't quite figure out, but it was worrying him. James smiled at the right moments, but it never seemed to reach his eyes. He told himself it was probably stress. It was a rough time at work for James, plus Dylan's graduation was looming. He needed to see if he could talk James into taking a weekend away. Not any place too fancy, but out of town, a step out of their lives for a moment.

———

THE SUN WAS STILL HIGH, and the afternoon fog had yet to roll in when Gabe parked across the street from James' building. It had been tempting to drive right past the turnoff and keep going north. They could head up to Napa or Calistoga and get drunk on good wine in a mud pool. Or maybe just hit the coast, then drive along Highway 1 until dark.

He looked over at James, who was staring out the window. "Busy week for both of us coming up, but I was thinking next weekend—"

"No," James said suddenly without turning around.

"Okay. If you've got something on then—"

"No." This time James did turn around. There was a quiver around his jaw as if he were trying not to cry. "We can't…. We shouldn't do this any… I shouldn't…." And with those fractured words, James jumped from the car, taking long, fast strides toward the security gate.

"Shit." Gabe leapt from his car and raced after James. "Whatever it is I'm really, really sorry, and I won't do it again, and please just tell me how I screwed up."

James didn't turn around, still a few steps ahead of him. "You didn't do anything wrong."

"I must have done something." Gabe caught up as James was punching in his security code. He grabbed James' arm but quickly dropped it, yanking his hand back, his heart racing. "Please just tell me?"

"You didn't—"

"It's the job, isn't it?" Gabe felt his throat begin to tighten. "I'm sorry, I lose focus, and please let me get through this week, and then I'm all yours. I swear. I'll shift my schedule. We'll get out of town—"

"No." James turned. "I—" Gabe saw James' mouth begin to form the words Gabe had been dying to hear and should have said first. James swallowed them back down. "You shouldn't be mine."

"What?"

"You do such amazing work." James swallowed hard a few times. "People depend on you. People's livelihoods, their lives, their families, depend on TechPrim, and TechPrim is yours, and everyone knows that. That's where your focus needs to be. What you do is so important to so many people, and it's going to continue to be important. You should keep your priorities and responsibilities right where they are. Where they need to be. You shouldn't let yourself become distracted by me and my little life."

Gabe tried desperately to compute what James was saying. He grabbed for James' hand. "And leaving me isn't going be distracting?"

"No," James whispered before quickly punching in his security code and disappearing behind the gate.

Gabe stood there for a long time. *He'll come back. He loves me, he almost said it, I could tell, he's just freaking out. He'll come back, and I'll say it, and he'll stop freaking out, and I fucking hate it when Frank is right. Should have said it right off. He loves me. He'll come back. Maybe this is just a nightmare. I'm exhausted. They get really realistic when I'm exhausted. How would I even know if I was dreaming?* Gabe bit his tongue, hard. On the rare occasions he had lucid nightmares, biting his tongue is what woke him up.

And older woman stepped around him carrying mesh grocery bags. The distinctive smell of fresh concha bread wafted up.

"Is the intercom not working again?" the woman asked. "I can let you through. I'm sure James is in this time of day."

"No," Gabe answered, despite an urge to bang on James' door and demand a better explanation. "I called," he lied. "We're meeting later."

Gabe rushed back to his car, still half hoping it was a dream. *Oh please let us meet later.*

INSIDE HIS HEAD James was screaming. It was a loud, long, pointless scream that soon became little more than white noise. The scream in his head was still going strong as he climbed the stairs, put the key in the lock, and opened the door.

"Hey, Dad." Dylan was on the couch with a history book.

"Hey." James could not handle anything beyond the most basic verbal communication at that moment.

Dylan popped up from the couch. "What the hell happened?"

"Nothing," he mumbled, heading directly toward his bedroom.

"Bullshit."

"Don't cuss." James was amazed he was able to form any words with the screaming in his head.

"You're crying."

"I'm not." James wasn't actually sure if that was a lie.

"What the fuck did Gabe do!"

"Nothing."

"Dad, tell me what he did. I'm going to call him and—"

"No! Leave him alone. He has to work. It's important."

It's important, it's important, James repeated to himself. *There are priorities. He doesn't need me and my—*

"Is *that* what he told you?" Dylan yelled. "Because if he used that as a lame-ass excuse—"

"I have a headache." That wasn't a lie. The back of his head was throbbing like he'd cracked it on something. "I think I'll lie down for a bit." Dylan tried to get in front of him, but he pushed past.

James walked down the hall to his room and sat on the bed. It squeaked. He put his hands over his ears as if that would somehow stop the screaming.

GABE WASN'T LISTENING. Some lawyer was talking at him. It was one of his own lawyers. There were also people from some other department in the meeting. He looked down at his notes. There were faxed and photocopied pages of Cyrillic with English translations handwritten under each line. He could barely read some of it. He bit down hard on his tongue and held it there. Nothing changed. That meant he was awake.

He glanced down at his phone. There were no messages. Nothing, despite a series of begging and apologetic messages he'd left for James when he'd gotten home on Saturday. Not that he had any faith those would help. After all, what do you say to a person who claims they would rather you focus on work?

He'd waited all weekend for a call or text or e-mail. The best he'd gotten was Dylan yelling at him. That had only stopped when he admitted he loved James. He had hoped that message would get passed along and he'd get something in return, but there was nothing.

He thumbed the map icon. James hadn't turned off the GPS on his phone. He possibly didn't even know it was a feature. A little picture of James' smiling face, flush with champagne, hovered over the UC Berkley campus. He knew what he was doing was weird, creepy, and maybe stalkerish, but he couldn't help it and didn't try to justify it.

He started on a text even as the lawyer droned on.

Is it someone else? I miss you already. You make me happy, did you know that? Do you really think you are that easy to forget or ignore? If there is someone else, please tell me. I want to know you're happy. I love you.

Some lawyer cleared his throat. Gabe looked up and hit delete on the message instead of send.

TAMYRA DROPPED a legal pad on his desk filled with her clean and bold handwriting. "Here, you can borrow my notes since you've obviously checked the fuck out."

"Sorry." Gabe had barely slept the previous night, his brain refusing to settle down, fighting contradictory information and creating horrible, convoluted plans for winning James back or justifying letting him go. The second one was starting to win. Experience had taught him that when someone chucked you out of their life, it was often safer to just go.

"Did you and James fight or something?"

"He left me," Gabe blurted out.

"What did you do?"

"Nothing!" Gabe shouted. "I didn't do anything. I… I was as attentive as possible, I respected his limits and choices, I respected the fuck out of *him*. I did my best." Gabe took a deep breath. "He walked away from me. He said he didn't want to distract me. That too many people relied on what I did, and he didn't want to take me away from that."

"And you bought that?"

Gabe laughed to keep from crying and pressed his forehead to his desk. "He was about to say he loved me. I could tell, and I should have listened to Frank and said it first and—" Gabe yanked himself up. "Sorry." He dragged a long breath through his teeth, gave himself a couple of hard mental slaps, then a physical one. "I'll get my head back in the game. I'll learn these notes. We're going to be fine. We're going to be fine, right?" He was pretty sure Tamyra would have at least elbowed him in the side if the meeting had been to tell him the deal had fallen through.

"We're going to be fine." Tamyra's voice was soft and steady, like a teacher calming a student. Gabe knew he was in trouble. "Virtually everything is settled, and I'm riding herd on the packs of lawyers. They're going to dig their heels in about a few things, but the odds of them walking away from the table are minimal."

"Thank you."

"You're welcome. Now have you begged James to take you back yet?"

"He's not answering my calls, but I've left a lengthy and very pathetic phone message. I'm waiting for a reply."

At that moment Gabe's office phone rang. He yanked it off the cradle, not bothering to check the caller ID. "James?"

"Gabriel."

Gabe's heart sank. "Hi, Mom. What do you need?"

JAMES CAME HOME to the smell of soup on the stove. It smelled like minestrone. There must have been a couple of cans in the cupboard.

Dylan came out from the kitchen. "Hey, Dad, I heated up some soup. Want some?"

"I'm not really hungry." In truth he hadn't eaten all day.

"Have you called Gabe back?"

James shook his head.

"You're both idiots. Come eat some soup."

GABE'S PHONE beeped with a message from Dylan.

You are both intractable idiots. Why aren't you begging him to come back?

"Because I already did, and he made his feelings on where my focus should be very clear when he walked away to begin with, and I'm trying to respect that," Gabe said aloud, to his empty office. His phone beeped again. This time it was from Tamyra, reminding him of a conference call he needed to dial into now.

Another message came in.

My party is still on Thursday. You are still invited.

JAMES TWISTED his phone around as he lay in his too-small bed, staring at the celling. He wondered if he should give the phone back. He was pretty sure that's what people did when they broke up: return the expensive gifts. But then the phone hadn't really been expensive. Gabe had probably gotten it for free.

He'd done some research, and in fact TechPrim had owed him a new phone. If it happened to be hand-delivered by the CFO of the company, who basically begged him to take it, then that was just the way it was.

He turned it on with a swipe of his thumb, the small screen illuminating the dark room. The background image was the one of himself and Gabe taken at the TechPrim birthday party. An official photographer for the evening had approached, and Gabe had swung an arm low around James' waist and pulled him close before smiling at the camera.

He looked through the gallery section for another picture to use as a background. He settled on a preloaded sunset. He'd left the picture of himself and Gabe up on his desktop at work, but that was only so his team didn't get suspicious. At least that's what he told himself.

13

Gabe was exhausted, and it was bothering him. He'd done more on far less sleep, and it hadn't hit him a fraction as hard compared to how he was feeling now. He flipped through the proposal document Tamyra had written, for the millionth time. Some of the dollar amounts had changed over the recent months, and there were a couple of new clauses, thanks to information the due-diligence guys had turned up, but it remained basically unchanged.

He fought back the urge to simply lay his head on his desk and slip into sleep. He tapped the map function on his phone. It showed James at home, but it also hadn't updated in twelve hours. So either James was home sick, or he'd turned off the GPS. Gabe had to admit he didn't really like either idea. He held his thumb over James' number: So easy to call again, but what would he say? Would James even pick up?

He shoved the phone away and turned back to the proposal.

"OKAY, come out here and let me see you."

Dylan stepped into the living room and gave a spin, showing off the dark green graduation gown.

"Put on the hat."

He grinned and settled the mortarboard onto his head, flipping the tassel to the side.

"Well, Dad. What do you think?"

James couldn't speak. He felt a tremble in one hand and a lump in his throat. He quickly blinked to keep his eyes clear. "You look really good," he managed to choke out. "God I'm proud of you."

"I'm not there yet."

"Still proud of you." James shifted the tassel around.

"How are you doing?" Dylan asked.

"I'm fine." James was lying of course, but the screaming in his head was not going to damage this day that they had worked so hard for.

"Liar."

"I am fine." He adjusted the way the robe sat on Dylan's shoulders and was reminded of Gabe adjusting his tux. "This is your day. You worry about you."

Dylan pinched his lips before giving James a quick hug. "Let's get going. I don't want to be late for this."

———

GABE WAS SWALLOWING two Tylenol and wondering what time Dylan's graduation might be and trying not to be depressed when Frank banged into the office.

"The negotiations are going fine. They're putting up a bit of a fuss about the properties in Yaroslavl, which we're giving them a perfectly good price for, but I think it's mainly an ego thing and—"

"Why am I just now finding out that you broke up with James?"

Gabe should have taken something stronger than Tylenol. Tequila maybe. Sales and marketing usually had alcohol. He could send down for some. "One, I don't know. Two, it's none of your business. Three, he walked out on me."

"What the hell did you do?"

"Why does everyone keep assuming it's my fault?" Gabe shouted. "He walked out on me. He decided that—" Gabe felt his throat pinch.

"Yeah. I got the gist from Tam." Frank leaned in close. "Gabe, my friend, why do you think I've been married three times?"

"Do you want an honest answer?"

Frank responded with a tight smile. "I've been married three times because I married the most perfect woman on earth when I was twenty-three and I let her walk away from me. We didn't fight, we didn't argue, she just didn't want to be in my way so she walked off, and I didn't go after her, I didn't even try, I put it off, I told myself she'd come back, and it is the stupidest thing I have ever done. Now she's married to a great guy, has a successful business, and has three beautiful kids that aren't mine, and if I thought for one second I could have her back, I would walk away from all of this. I'd leave you, Nate, I'd burn TechPrim to the fucking ground if it meant having Claire back for even one day."

Gabe stared at Frank, unsure what to say. He remembered Claire. He had liked Claire—everyone had liked Claire—and when she walked out, Frank had spent a couple of days drunk and then got back to work. They'd had deadlines to meet. "I have to be in a meeting," is what Gabe finally said.

"You need to take a close look at your priorities, and don't be a fucking moron."

THE SPEECHES HAD BEEN GIVEN by the principal, the valedictorian, and some guy who'd graduated forty years before and had been dragged back to give some out-of-date life advice. James gripped his mother's hand tighter than was probably comfortable, but he couldn't help it. The graduates stood and filed forward as each name was called.

"He's going to be fine," his mother whispered.

"I know." And he did, but that knowledge didn't slow down his heart, which was racing in his chest. Technically it would be Dylan's second time across a graduation stage. When James was graduating, Dylan had a summer cold and had been going through a clingy phase. He made a break for it during the valedictorian speech and rushed the stage. James' classmates had simply scooped him up, passed him two rows back and plopped him into James' lap. James ended up getting his diploma with Dylan on his hip, rubbing snot into the shoulder of his gown. At the time it had felt strangely appropriate and only the valedictorian, some Harvard-bound kiss ass, complained about having his speech upstaged.

Catherine's name was called, and Dylan jumped to his feet, applauding. Her hair was dyed the same green as her graduation gown.

A half dozen students later, the vice principal got to the *M* names. "Dylan Maron."

James jumped to his feet, applauding for all he was worth and refusing to cry. Dylan took long, sure strides across the stage, took the diploma, shook the principal's hand, and tossed a smile to the crowd. James kept applauding even as Dylan circled around back to his seat.

Later, as the families milled around outside the school auditorium, James pulled Dylan into another hug. "I am so proud of you."

"It's just high school, Dad."

"Turn around, you two," James' mom called out. "It's time for pictures."

ONE OF A DOZEN lawyers droned on as Gabe glanced down at his phone. He was sure they were talking about something that had already been settled, but it was as if no one wanted the responsibility of actually being the one to agree.

He flicked open an image file sent from Dylan, despite the lump it dropped into his stomach.

In the picture Dylan was in his graduation robes, his arm around James' shoulder, and flanked by an older couple that he guessed must be James' parents.

Who's missing from this picture? You need to think up something better to say because every day is another day he can convince himself he was right. You're breaking his heart and I'm considering breaking your legs. You're still invited tomorrow. Good luck with the Russians.

Gabe looked up at the Russians and choked down the mix of anger and pain that settled into his throat.

PAPERWORK COVERED NEARLY every inch of Gabe's coffee table, but he was ignoring it. Instead he was staring at the picture Dylan had sent for the hundredth time when his intercom buzzed. It was such a rare occurrence, he jumped a little, and his heart began to race, because maybe it was James. Maybe James sent Dylan off to some graduation party, then drove down. He rushed to the panel by the elevator.

"Hello?"

"It's Margaret. Let me up."

Gabe's heart sank even as he wondered what Margaret was doing.

"Come on up."

A minute later the elevator doors whooshed open nearly silently. Margaret stepped out with a couple of Tupperware containers and a bottle of wine. "I brought you dinner."

"Thanks. I was going to—"

"Order takeout or something? God knows how you keep your figure." She bustled into the kitchen and scrounged up some plates and a couple of wine glasses. "Where do you keep your corkscrew?"

"The left drawer. I really shouldn't be drinking—"

"Yes, you should."

"I've got—"

"Do you really believe you're going to get your head around all that Russian law in the next twelve hours when you've had months to learn it?"

"Are you going to let me finish a sentence?"

"Not until you start saying things I want to hear." She yanked the cork out of a bottle of red. She filled one glass to the brim and pushed it toward Gabe.

"Red wine gives me hangovers."

"I know. Drink that anyway while I put dinner on the plate."

"You didn't come over just to feed me, did you?"

"Nope. Drink, eat, then talk."

Dinner was a thick beef stew with still-warm, soft french bread, eaten on Gabe's couch.

"How many guys have walked out on you?" Margaret asked once the bowls had been licked clean and the wine glasses refilled.

Gabe only thought for a second before giving up trying to count. "I don't know. Do you?"

"Yes, in fact, I do. And when is the last time you actually chased after one?"

"If someone leaves it's for a reason."

"That doesn't answer my question, and there is a difference

between reasons and good reasons. And from what I've gathered, James gave you a crap reason because I can guarantee he's terrified and doesn't know what he's doing."

"I've heard this speech already."

"Then why haven't you gone after him?"

"I've left some very pathetic messages explaining how I feel, and I've had…." Gabe waved his hand at the stack of documents sitting on his coffee table. "Which is what he *wants* me to be focusing on, I'd like to add."

"Then show him you can multitask." Margaret took his hand. "I haven't seen you happy in a long time. Not properly happy." Gabe didn't want to think about the last time someone really made him happy. "You built an empire on a long shot of a crazy idea of Frank and my husband's. You kick yourself any time any competitor develops *anything* before TechPrim. But you aren't willing to chase down someone who makes you happy."

"Last time—"

"Don't!" Margaret snapped. "Do not. Gregory was ages ago, and you need to stop letting his ghost fuck up your personal life. He was a bad person doing bad things to you and to your company but that is not an excuse to let James go. TechPrim is safe. You are safe. You are in a safe position to risk a little happiness in your life. You can't keep using him as an excuse. You can't keep using TechPrim as an excuse."

Gabe leaned back into his sofa and stared at the ceiling with its dark wood panels that he had spent weeks choosing. He tried to let his mind go blank because it was better than dwelling on mistakes past and present.

Thinking back over the long, storied history of Margaret and Nate's "courtship," Gabe leaned forward. "Margaret, why did you force feed Nate a worm?"

"Because he pulled my hair one day when it was raining, and he pulled too hard. I fell backward into a puddle, at which point I got very angry, jumped up, chased him, tackled him to the ground, and shoved an unlucky worm into his mouth that had crawled up onto the sidewalk."

"I always wondered. Never got around to asking. He still fell in love with you?"

"After I fed him the worm, I got up and went to the boy who had bullied him into pulling my hair, and I punched him in the face. Knocked out one of his baby teeth." Gabe laughed despite the tightness that seemed to have permanently moved into his chest. "I had some anger management issues as a small child."

"Obviously." Gabe downed the last of his wine. "It was Dylan's graduation today."

"James must be very proud."

"James is thirty-two. He's younger than I am. He could be bringing pictures of grandbabies to his next high school reunion."

"So could you."

"That's getting ahead of things."

"I know you, Gabe. Your brain runs a century in advance. Look me in the eye, and tell me you haven't worked out a life with James right down to grandkids running around some house by the sea."

Gabe's squeezed his eyes shut before he cried. "Get the fuck out of my brain."

"Only if you start using it."

14

The words "Dylan's Party" crawled closer to the top of Gabe's rolling agenda. He stared at it as they were taking a break. No one seemed willing to take the responsibility of saying yes to a very good deal and Gabe couldn't understand why. They were down to arguing minutiae and pointing out obscure clauses in Russian business law that may or may not even apply. If Gabe was honest with himself, he'd lost track of the details by ten that morning. When a break was called, he hadn't even had the energy to trek back up to his office. Instead he flopped down in an unused cubicle.

Tamyra had followed him, but whatever she had been saying had become little more than a white noise. His phone pinged at him reminding him of the party. He glanced outside. It was a beautiful, bright early June day. There were a few fluffy clouds, and the smog wasn't too thick yet.

"I don't want to be here."

"What?"

"What?" Gabe realized he must have said that thought out loud. He stared at Tamyra in her perfect suit, perfect shoes, and perfectly coordinated jewelry, while contemplating the words that had just slipped from his mouth.

I don't want to be here.

"Tam, you know this deal, right?"

"Yes." Tamyra stretched out the word.

"I mean, you know it better than I do. You wrote that damn proposal, you've got your head around the international law."

"Yeah."

"And I've got a small army of exceedingly well-paid international business lawyers sitting in that room, right?" Gabe's heart began to speed up.

"Last I checked."

"Good." Out the window Gabe could see the trees swaying slightly in a soft breeze. He rose to his feet. His hands shook. "You're fired."

Tamyra laughed.

"No, I'm serious. You're fired. You're not my PA anymore."

"Are you feeling okay? Do you need me to call Dr. Gowda?" She pressed the back of her hand to his forehead then felt along the sides of his neck and behind his ears.

He rolled whatever piece of paper was in his hand into a tube and tapped it to her shoulders. "I hereby dub you Vice President of International Acquisition. Your first order is to explain to the people in that room that I've had something come up. Then nail down that deal so I can spend tomorrow night getting drunk on vodka."

"You're serious, aren't you?" For the first time in their ten years together, Gabe saw a shadow of fear on Tamyra's usually carefully composed face.

"Yes, I am. And once you've got this deal done, hire two new PAs, one for me and one for yourself. Also write yourself up a contract and stick it on my desk. I'll sign it and send it down to human resources."

"You're really serious, I mean—"

He giggled for no reason he could pinpoint, but it felt good. "Time to start loosening the death grip a little."

Tamyra took a very deep breath, and Gabe could see her count slowly to five before letting it out. "You're picking one fucking hell of a time to do it."

"I have faith in you. Now I need to get out of here."

"Okay." There was actually a slight squeak in her voice. "There's something sitting under my desk that you're going to need if you're going where I think you're going."

Gabe gave her a kiss on the cheek. "You are the best and always will be. Now go talk a bunch of Russians into taking my money."

THE TREES WERE FILLED with bright crepe paper streamers. James wondered if he had gone a bit overboard. It had been several years since he'd done a party where streamers or balloons were involved, but his mother had insisted.

He supposed it was too late now. Catherine had already arrived, as well as Coach Frasier and a few of Dylan's friends. They were gathering together around the barbecue his father was manning. In the distance he could hear the carousel music start again. It had been years since he'd heard the tune banged out by the antique mechanized band, but it existed in the background of many good memories.

He shoved his hands in his pockets. He ran his fingers across the smooth lines of his phone.

He wondered how Gabe's negotiations were going. He couldn't help picturing them happening down in some Cold War bunker, a map spread across the table as men in large fuzzy hats whispered to each other. But it was probably in some light, airy TechPrim conference room. There was a breeze rustling the long eucalyptus trees. He remembered a walk on the beach he and Gabe had taken once and the way the sea breeze had blown Gabe's curls in all directions.

A bright blue balloon got loose from one of the tables and started bouncing across the rough grass. James chased after it before it popped or blew into the wild blackberry brambles, thick with still-green fruit. He managed to snatch it up off the ground before it hit the gravel path.

He looked up. A tall blonde woman approached him. It took him a moment to recognize her. The last time he'd seen her, Dylan had been fifteen, and some therapist had told her she should try to reconnect with her son. She'd had long honey-blonde hair, the same shade as Dylan's. Now it was cropped short but stylish.

"Cindy." He kept his voice as neutral as possible.

"James." She gave a slight nod. "And before you ask, Dylan invited me. So I figure we can be civil for a few hours. For his sake?"

"I think I can manage."

"So." She tilted her head back and stared into the pale blue sky. "He's eighteen."

"Yes, he is."

"Doesn't seem that long ago."

"I know."

Cindy shifted her eyes from the sky to the ground where she kicked a couple of eucalyptus nuts. "I've been thinking a lot over the last couple of months about everything that happened, and I want to say I'm sorry."

Those were the last words that James expected to come out of her mouth. Their relationship had been downright hostile for years. "There were two of us there. I might have been drunk, but I remember that much."

"No, not about that. I shouldn't have listened to my parents. They… they told me you wouldn't care. That you'd be relieved and just move on, and I knew…. They never thought for one moment that you'd put up a fight. Not like you did. But I knew that if anyone would have fought, it would have been you."

James felt his pulse kick up and his adrenaline begin to flow. Even after all this time, thinking about those days got him worked up.

"I shouldn't have listened to them," Cindy continued. "And I keep thinking that maybe if we had just talked to you... If we'd all sat down and taken some time, found a couple that weren't religious weirdos, maybe a couple nearby that would have let us visit, be involved, maybe you wouldn't have needed to give up all you did."

"I didn't—"

"James." She cut him off. "I still talked to people after I transferred. The teachers let you sleep in class as long as you kept a C average. You were so much better than that. Maybe if we'd—"

"Don't do this, Cindy." James didn't want the reminders. Not on this day. "Believe me, you start going down the whole woulda, coulda, shoulda path, you'll go nuts, really quick. I made my choices. I lived with them. And that's what life is."

She looked past him to where Dylan was talking with some of his friends. "You did a good job with him."

"I did my best." James tried to calm himself. Truthfully the last thing he had ever expected from Cindy was an apology.

"Your best is pretty damn good. Better than most."

"I've got a guy at work who thinks I should write a book, *The Stupid Teenager's Guide to Parenting.*"

"I'd read it."

"We'll see what happens." James waved to a well-loaded picnic table, balloon still in hand. "We've got plenty of food and some wine for the grown-ups."

"Actually, I'm not drinking right now." Cindy bit her lip and closed her eyes. "I'm pregnant."

"You're…. Really?" James couldn't keep the surprise out of his voice or off his face.

"Yes, my husband and I decided it was time to do it properly, as it were."

James looked her over. She didn't look particularly far in. "How long?"

"Four months."

"Does Dylan know?" It's something Dylan would have kept from him, fully aware of his parents' relationship.

"No. It's his birthday. I don't want to drop something like that on him."

"He'd be thrilled."

"You think so?"

"I know so. When he was six, we had to have a very interesting conversation about why he wasn't getting a baby brother, sister, or puppy any time soon."

"Puppy?"

"It was an interesting conversation."

"Thank you, James. I mean it."

James shrugged slightly, completely unsure as to what to say. Cindy patted him on the arm and headed toward Dylan. James stayed where he was, watching from a distance. Dylan was well past noncustodial kidnapping age, but it was still a deeply ingrained paranoia, and it was hard to see him near his mother or any member of her family without feeling a twinge of it. He watched as they hugged briefly. James told himself it was a good thing. A child should have a positive relationship with both parents. There seemed to be a bit of small talk, and then Dylan's face split into a grin. He pulled his mother into a much tighter hug, then spread his hand across her stomach.

James quietly hoped it was a boy. Dylan had really wanted a baby brother but was willing to settle for a sister. Actually he'd wanted a puppy more than a sibling. A few more of Dylan's friends were strolling across the grass. James waved at them before heading back to reattach the balloon.

GABE HOPPED out of the car at the edge of a steep lawn stretching up to the Tilden Park merry-go-round. A large, brightly wrapped gift, addressed to Dylan (that he'd found under Tamyra's desk per her instructions), was tucked under his arm. Just beyond he could see picnic tables with some people milling around and balloons taped to trees. He froze. Yes, he'd been invited by Dylan, but James had uninvited him from his entire life. He turned to go back to the car, but Jared was making shooing motions, and to drive the point home, he pulled away from the curb and sped off.

Gabe turned back around and marched toward his destiny, occasionally stepping around some dog poo and an ant hill. Once he got close enough to see the "Congratulations Dylan" sign, he yanked off his tie, knowing he was still supremely overdressed. He set his gift with the others and scanned the crowd. There were a handful of teenagers but also several adults. A few people looked his way, but no one approached.

He spotted James near a grill. Before he could make a decision as to a next move, James spotted him. There really was no turning back. He smiled, waved a little, and managed to meet James around the edge of the party.

"Hi." He wanted to pull James into a kiss, but James had stopped a polite distance from him, folding his hands behind his back. "Dylan invited me. Can we talk for a quick second?"

James looked around, seeming to scan the party for an excuse to say no. "Sure. Don't you have some billion-dollar deal going down today?" It wasn't accusatory, just a question.

"It's a second-stage negotiation, and Tamyra's handling it. I've made her a VP and tossed her into the pool."

James frowned. "Why?"

"Because she's more than earned it, she knows the finer details of the deal better than I do, she's probably a better person to negotiate at this stage in the proceedings, and I was invited to a birthday party."

"You can't—" James began.

"I'm the boss. Yes, I can. Please. Just... I need to say some things." Gabe took a deep breath. He'd spent the drive rehearsing declarations of love and sweet promises. "How dare you," is what came out.

James started, as did Gabe, at the anger that suddenly bubbled up. "You don't get to tell me what I need or what my priorities should be or what I should consider important. I am an adult, and you don't get to decide that what I feel for you should be worth less than my job."

"But—"

"No," Gabe cut in. "No. You said you didn't want to distract me. I have been nothing but distracted. Look." Gabe held up his hands, displaying fingers chewed until they bled. James' eyes went wide. "I can't stop gnawing on them. I even tried the vanilla. And since the moment you walked away I've had people telling me I'm an idiot and a coward for not chasing after you because I'm never going to do better than you, and they are right, even if you don't believe it."

He took a couple of deep breaths, trying to slow his racing heart but to no avail. "I need someone in my life. I need *you* in my life. I want you in my life. You are the strongest person I have ever met and really one of the best people I know and... you humble me. Since the first day I met you I knew you weren't like anyone else. And I need you to know that you are a priority in my life, and I get to decide what my priorities should be."

"Gabe, you have a multi*billion*-dollar deal happening today." James' voice was pained.

"Yes, I do. And I will have to fly to Moscow and get alcohol poisoning to finalize it. But I also have a *vast* team of brilliant people from the best business schools and poached from the best companies who could take at least half my job off my plate, but I won't let them. They sit on their asses and collect big paychecks. Doing it all myself is an unnecessary habit that has been eating my life away for years. And, yes, TechPrim's my baby, but my baby is older than your baby, and for my own sake, just like you, I need to start prying my hands off."

Gabe felt the anger begin to fade, only to be replaced by heartsick pain. "And I want to be an important part of your life. I won't be able to change things overnight, my life is locked into some pretty set patterns, but I want a reason to try. I have *missed* you so much. A lot of people have walked out on me, but you are the first one in a long time I have missed."

James was blinking at him, his mouth slightly open, and his face giving little twitches. "You—" He swallowed hard.

"I love you." The words tumbled from Gabe's mouth, and there was no taking them back. The shock registered on James' face. He hoped James would say those same words in return, but he didn't expect them. Even if James did love him.

"You're serious, aren't you?"

"Yes I am. Now if you don't want me in your life because I work crazy hours and way too much and will be constantly rescheduling date nights, or if you honestly don't feel anything for me, please tell me now, and I'll go. But I really do... I really do love you and... I want you to take me camping. It sounds like fun."

"It is." James' voice was nearly a whisper. "You love me?"

"I will prove it." Gabe took out his phone. "I will turn this off."

James grabbed his hand. Gabe could feel them shaking just as they had that afternoon on the bridge when he had first pulled James into a kiss. "You've got a multi*billion*-dollar deal going down today. Leave it on."

Gabe slid the phone back into his pocket. "Is that a yes? Should I stay?"

"That's a—" James chewed on his lip. "I... I've missed you too."

Gabe glanced over James' shoulder. Dylan was staring at them while leaning casually on a baseball bat. The mixture of fear and relief was a heady one.

"Can I kiss you? Please?"

"Yes," James answered instantly.

Gabe stepped in close and pressed their lips together so softly it was nearly chaste. It was James who deepened the kiss and wrapped his arms around Gabe. He felt the horrible knots that had been living between his shoulders and deep in his throat for nearly a week simply vanish. He held James tight and perhaps a little longer than was appropriate given the occasion, but he really didn't care. It was James who finally pulled away but pressed their foreheads together.

"I don't ever want to go more than twenty-four hours without doing that again," Gabe whispered to him.

James smiled and flushed. Forget twenty-four hours. Gabe never wanted to go more than one hour without seeing that smile again. He glanced over James' shoulder to see the entire party staring at them. There was one particular older couple who were whispering frantically to each other. "We have an audience."

"I know." James' eyes were fixed over Gabe's shoulder on the merry-go-round. "That's why I haven't turned around yet."

"Am I going to be meeting your parents in the next two minutes?"

"Most likely."

Gabe did a quick once-over on himself: nice suit, clean shoes, brushed teeth, some standard sleep deprivation but nothing he couldn't bluff his way through. "Okay. As long as there's no mescal involved, I'm sure all will be fine."

"Very unlikely." James straightened out his shirt, ran a quick hand down the front of Gabe's, and turned to face the party.

JAMES STROLLED TOWARD HIS PARENTS, his head high and his cheeks burning. Gabe loved him. That was the only real thought that existed now. Gabe loved him. Gabe got angry at him and came back. Gabe loved him and was there by his side instead of hammering out a major deal. James tried to feel guilty about that, but it was hard because Gabe loved him. Gabe had offered to turn off his phone. Gabe loved him, and he loved Gabe. But he hadn't said it back. He'd wanted to, but the words got stuck somehow. He would have to unstick them, soon, by the end of the day.

He smiled as he approached his parents. "Mom, Dad, this is Gabe Juarez, my boyfriend. Gabe, these are my parents, Leslie and Arthur Maron."

Gabe put on one of those truly dazzling smiles of his as he held out his hand. "It's a pleasure to meet you both."

"It's nice to meet you too," James' mother replied sweetly.

"Finally," his father added, directing it toward James.

"Dad," James hissed.

"And it's so good of you to come. I'm sure you must be busy," James' mother continued as if nothing else had been said.

"What good is being the boss and working crazy hours if you can't occasionally take a summer afternoon off?" Suddenly Gabe's phone started playing "Genie in a Bottle." He ignored it. "Besides, it's Dylan's eighteenth birthday. I thought James could use the emotional support."

James reached up and touched his arm. "It's Tamyra, you can get it."

Gabe cringed. "I'm sorry, this'll just take a second." He slipped out his phone and took a few steps away.

"'Genie in a Bottle'?" his father asked, looking unimpressed.

"His PA put it on his phone as her ringtone so he'll answer it quickly. Every time he takes it off she puts on something worse. When we first met it was 'Dancing Queen.'"

His father nodded. "That's sort of ingenious."

"Tamyra's pretty awesome. The TechPrim PAs are running the company with an iron fist."

Dylan approached as Gabe got off the phone. "Hey, Gabe, glad you could make it." His tone was casual, but his eyes were still hard as he looked over Gabe. And he was still holding a bat.

"I would have been stupid to miss it."

"How are things with the Russians?"

"Well." Gabe looked down at the phone still in his hand. "I should have promoted Tamyra to VP years ago and put her in charge of the whole thing months ago because after I left she walked back into the negotiations, told them to cut the crap, and the second-stage contracts will be ready for me to sign bright and early tomorrow morning. All that's left is to go to Moscow in a few months and try to survive alcohol poisoning."

Dylan raised a cup of soda. "Congratulations."

EVERYONE STARTED MOVING toward the food even as Gabe continued to make small talk with James' parents, answering questions about himself, his family, his job. A few of the questions from Arthur Maron were blunt and a bit pointed, but Gabe was well aware he was the first boyfriend James had "brought home" as it were, so he was going to be on the receiving end of years of denied parental interrogation. He did manage to slip in a few times what an amazing man he thought James was and what a great grandson they had as well. That seemed to go a long way toward making a good impression.

When he noticed Dylan heading for seconds on food, he excused himself and followed quickly, managing to cut Dylan off from the crowd. "Happy birthday."

"Thanks. I'm glad you came."

"So am I. How's your ankle?" The way Dylan had been leaning on his bat would have taken the weight off his injured leg.

"It'll hold," Dylan answered without emotion.

"Good. Your official present is on the table. I don't actually know what it is. Tam picked it out. I think it's a laptop."

Dylan grinned. "I will happily accept one of those. Thank you!"

"Figured you might. I got your dad's okay for it. I also have an unofficial gift for you. Between you and me so your dad doesn't get weird." Gabe slipped Dylan the check he'd written in the car.

Dylan looked at it and simply blinked for several seconds. "Seriously?"

"I went to college on scholarship too. They say everything is covered, but there are always incidentals. If nothing else, the week before finals when you've been up for three days banging out twenty-page papers, it doesn't matter how broke you are, you *will* order pizza."

"That's a lot of pizza."

"You're good with a budget. I'm sure you can stretch that over four years."

"That's still a lot of pizza. I… I don't know if I can take this." Dylan was still staring at the check. Gabe was unsurprised by the Maron pride.

"Then consider it a long-term, interest-free loan."

Dylan stared at it for several more seconds before he

carefully folded the check and slipped it into his pocket. Then he held out his hand. "Thank you."

"No, thank you. And before the Major League career kicks off, TechPrim is always looking for good young minds."

"Not afraid I'd come after your job?"

Gabe grinned. "I'd be disappointed if you didn't."

JAMES LOOKED over his shoulder to see Gabe and Dylan shaking hands. He let out a breath of relief he didn't know he'd been holding. Dylan had been a bit of a grouch the last few days and refused to stop hovering, asking James every five minutes how he was feeling.

Gabe came back to the table with a second hot dog as Dylan went around to the front of the tables, a cup in his hand.

"Hi, everyone. Can I just say something quick here, before we get to cake?" The conversation died down as people turned Dylan's way. "I know this isn't the usual eighteen blowout, but I guess I have some stuff I want to say, and it's easier if I can get you all in one place. I know this sounds weird, but I've got a bunch of people I need to thank. First, Mom, I know things have been odd between us, but you brought me into this world, so that counts for a lot. I need to thank Steve Sanderson, attorney-at-law, without whom I would be one of *literally* Jesus-only-knows how many kids. Grandma and Grandpa, you were always there for Dad and me when things got rough or when we just couldn't handle one more night of Dad's cooking. Coach Frasier, you put a bat in my hand when I was eight and told me it could take me places. Well, it's taking me to Stanford, so I've got to thank you for that. And mostly I've got to thank my dad. He had the ultimate guilt card up his sleeve my entire life, and he never once used it. He simply made a decision and soldiered on every day to try to make my life the best it could be, give me as many options as possible. I know he's been worried about getting me to eighteen without a criminal record, eating disorder, pyromaniac tendencies, unplanned offspring, drug addictions, any major antisocial behaviors, zombie apocalypse, or alien abductions. Well, Dad, you did it. You dragged us both across the finish line, and for that I will always owe you." Dylan raised his cup, and James wiped his eyes. "Thank you."

Everyone raised their cups even as James ducked his head. It seemed to be a day for embarrassment. He gave Dylan's shoulder a squeeze as he sat back down. James started on a second burger.

"You should save some room for cake," Gabe said.

James laughed. "I will always have room for cake." A certain giddiness had come over him. He was sitting outside on a perfect summer day. The air was filled with bird song, crickets, tinny carousel music, and the sharp smell of the eucalyptus. His grown son was on one side of him, his boyfriend was warm on the other, and his parents were across from him. He could hear people talking and laughing all around him. He knew it was Dylan's special day, but for the first time, possibly ever, everything in his life was feeling right.

Gabe leaned in close. "You look happy."

"I think I am."

"Happy looks good on you."

"Yeah." There was just one thing missing. James took a deep breath and leaned in close, pressing his lips to Gabe's ear. "I love you too."

EPILOGUE

Mornings in the high Sierras are cold and clear, even in late July. Gabe wiggled himself out of the small tent and squinted into the early light. A few birch trees were reflected in the glassy stillness of the lake where he and James had pitched their tent two days earlier. He took a couple of deep breaths as he bent backwards, feeling his spine pop and crack. Logically, he knew the air was thinner, but with every breath he'd swear there was actually more oxygen in it. Or maybe his head was clearing because the sunlight didn't need to fight its way through the fog and the smog.

James was asleep, the years of stress having melted away in the clean mountain air, giving him more peace than any sleeping pill or relaxation therapy. Gabe, on the other hand, was still decompressing, his internal clock waking him in time for international conference calls he didn't have. And there was a bird with a high trilling song that sounded just a little too close to the TechPrim default ringtone. That would have to change when he got back.

He reminded himself that anyone of any importance knew exactly where he was and that there were ways of getting ahold of him. They were only a six-hour drive from home if he was really needed. If something completely went to shit, there was a seldom used but functional TechPrim helicopter which could make the trip in half the time.

He took another deep breath of icy air and turned his face to the sun.

The old propane powered camping stove was still set up from their dinner the night before. James had insisted on providing the camping equipment instead of letting Gabe purchase everything new. That meant the stove had seen better days and the tent had patches of duct tape here and there. Gabe had put his foot down on one front and bought new sleeping bags and air mattresses. If this was going to be the first proper vacation he or James had taken in years, they were going to sleep comfortably.

The propane hissed from the little burner as Gabe held out a match at arm's length. He was hardly more than a generation removed from half-starved migrant farmworkers who survived in far harsher conditions, but that didn't mean he wasn't a total city boy and more than a little afraid of blowing something up while trying to light a thirty-year-old stove.

There was a soft fwump as the gas caught. The day would turn blazing hot by ten, but for the next couple of hours it would be chilly enough to warrant a hot breakfast, or at least hot coffee.

He was warming his hands around a steaming cup of instant coffee, the smell drowning him in nostalgia as it was the only kind his mother ever drank, when he heard the tent flaps rustle. James poked his head out, squinting into the light. His hair was sticking out in every possible direction, still mussed from the previous night's activities. He looked like he could easily fall back asleep. Instead he crawled from the tent.

"Coffee?"

James nodded.

"You got the stove working."

"Fingers and eyebrows still attached."

James' responding smile was soft and still a little sleepy. Then he gave Gabe a small kiss which lingered and slowly deepened. Gabe put one arm around his waist and pulled him close. He could feel the first hints of stubble on James' lip. That was new. Before Gabe could muse on that much more, James slipped the coffee from Gabe's hands, took a small sip, then handed it back. "I'll start breakfast."

Like Gabe, James was having his own problems breaking years of habit. Unlike Gabe, James' habits leaned more to the domestic. While James cracked a few eggs into a dented aluminum frying pan, Gabe tried not to think about the fact that his phone was locked in the car with a nearly flat battery. While he could possibly get a text or quick call through, there was zero data coverage so no emails or news. He briefly wondered if perhaps TechPrim should branch out into the telecommunication service provider side of things, but that would mean even more dealings with the FCC.

He chided himself for thinking about work on what was supposed to be proper vacation time. It had only been a couple of months since he'd promised to start delegating his responsibilities. At times it had been like detoxing with the guys or Tamyra physically blocking him from meetings he didn't need to be in and shoving him in his car at six. Orders to go see James had usually taken the worst of the fight out of him. He took a moment to look James up and down then went to help him with the eggs.

"What would you like to do today?" James asked once breakfast was nearly finished. "It's going to get hot."

James' had pointed out that July was not the ideal time to visit the eastern Sierras, but it was the earliest time they had matching vacation days and Gabe was determined to go as part of his campaign to not work himself into an early grave.

"What would you recommend?"

"Well, we could go up to Mono Lake. See the tufa cones and the sand flies. If you're up for a longer drive, there's the Bodie ghost town. Haven't been there since I was a Kid."

There was a shift in the breeze and Gabe could feel the first kiss of heat in the air. They had agreed to take a whole week off, their friends insisting that a weekend away didn't count. He'd checked the weather before leaving and it was supposed to cool down a little later in the week. Not that it wouldn't be blazing hot, but it might drop to something tolerable enough to go hiking across desert salt beaches.

"Or," James said, noticing Gabe's delay in responding, "We can move our camp chairs under those trees, do some reading, make out a bit, then jump in the lake when it gets really hot. And after that, take a nap?"

"I did pack a book." An actual, printed-on-paper, work of fiction, book.

"I know. So did I." James grinned at him and he grinned back.

"I think our friends would be proud of us if we spent at least some of our vacation just sitting under a tree, reading."

END

Ada Maria Soto is a Mexican/American expat living in the South Pacific. She's a veteran of the theatre and film business as well as all the lousy jobs that come with two liberal arts degrees. A psychologist once told her she has a fantasy prone personality, but since she's trying to be a writer that's not a bad thing. She is a fan of rugby, cricket, and baseball, who loves to cook, knit, and poke around her garden. She loves to hear from her fans, or really anyone who has read her work.

Join her newsletter to stay up to date with new releases.

https://adamariasoto.com

ALSO BY ADA MARIA SOTO